Mr. Darcy to the Rescue
A Pride and Prejudice Variation

By Victoria Kincaid

This is a work of fiction. Names, characters, places, and incidents are products of the author's imagination or are used fictitiously. Any resemblance to actual events or persons, living or dead, is entirely coincidental.

ISBN: 978-0-9916681-4-4

Chapter 1

"…And now nothing remains for me but to assure you in the most animated language of the violence of my affection!"

It must be admitted that Elizabeth Bennet's attention had drifted a little as her cousin, Mr. Collins, had enumerated at great length his reasons for choosing to marry and why he had very rationally selected Elizabeth for this "honor."

Now as Elizabeth focused on his words, she had to stifle a laugh at the idea that his affection for her was violent or deep or anything more than nonexistent. In fact, he had not even managed to produce any "animated language." Instead, he had merely assured her that his language was animated. It was a bit like having someone declare it was raining when you stood in bright sunshine.

Oh, merciful heavens, he was still talking! "To fortune I am perfectly indifferent, and you may assure yourself that no ungenerous reproach shall ever pass my lips when we are married." As he drew breath for another long-winded speech, Elizabeth knew she must say something—and quickly!

"You are too hasty, sir! You forget that I have not yet made an answer—"

Mr. Collins waved his hand airily. "We may dispense with these formalities. We both know how you shall respond."

"We do?" Elizabeth expected smoke to be streaming from her ears by now.

"Yes, I have spoken with your most excellent father, and he assured me how felicitous he found this event." He graced her with a smile, which presumably was intended to be charming, but oozed insincerity.

"He did?" Elizabeth found these words hard to credit.

"Indeed. I assured him that our union is already a foregone conclusion since we are united of one mind and one heart."

"We are?" Elizabeth could not stay silent any longer. "Pray, sir, when did that happen?"

Mr. Collins merely looked bemused. "I...do not believe I can supply you with the exact date...."

Elizabeth shrugged. "I keep a journal. I shall have to go back to see if I recorded it." She tapped her lip with her finger. "I hope it did not escape my notice."

Her erstwhile suitor blinked rapidly, fiddling with his cuffs. "Your father did caution me that you should speak with him first before making any decision regarding my most generous offer." He shrugged. "I do not see the necessity since we both know that another offer of marriage may never be made to you... Miss Elizabeth?"

Mr. Collins had been so caught up in the sound of his own voice that it took him a few moments to realize that Elizabeth was halfway across the drawing room floor. He hastened to catch up with her. "Where are you going, my most precious love blossom?"

The sound of this ridiculous pet name almost stopped Elizabeth altogether, but she had a more urgent mission. "I must speak with my father," she muttered.

"Why?"

"To assure myself his wits are in order."

"Hmm?" Mr. Collins's tone was quizzical. "I assure you he was of quite sound mind this morning when I spoke to him."

Briefly, Elizabeth considered the possibility that Mr. Collins was so stupid he was incapable of being insulted. Elizabeth would be tempted to laugh if the situation were not so dire. Why would her father give Mr. Collins the impression he wanted her to marry him?

She opened the door to her father's study rather more forcefully than she intended, and it banged against the wall. Her father looked up from his desk as Elizabeth closed the door, preventing Mr. Collins from entering.

"Ah, Lizzy, I thought I might receive a visit from you." Elizabeth's father removed his spectacles and regarded his daughter with a grim smile.

Elizabeth sat in the chair opposite the desk but perched on the edge, unable to relax. She expected Papa to smile and laugh or at least regard her with an ironic twinkle in his eye. Instead, he merely looked worn and solemn. "Mr. Collins has made me an offer of marriage." Her voice trembled with uncertainty.

"And you listened to him?"

"I suppose I must be amenable to people's wishes some of the time, or I run the danger of becoming predictable."

Such banter usually drew a chuckle from her father, but today, it merely produced a rather wan smile. Fingers of anxiety crept up Elizabeth's spine. "Papa, is there something amiss?"

Her father's hands fiddled with his spectacles. "The last thing I wanted was to burden you with this. If Mr. Bingley had… Well, it is of no matter."

Elizabeth said nothing. Everyone in the family had been disappointed when Mr. Bingley had abruptly left the neighborhood two days earlier. Jane tried to hide her melancholy, but the loss still haunted her eyes. Elizabeth still believed that Mr. Bingley would return, but his sister's latest letter to Jane had held little hope.

Papa rubbed his hand over his forehead wearily. "Do you recall when Mr. Bartlett was here a week ago?" Elizabeth nodded. She had sent for the doctor herself after her father experienced pains in his chest. "I may have misled your mother about how severe he believes the problem to be."

Elizabeth's breath caught.

"Mr. Bartlett believes my heart is weakening. And it is only a matter of time until it fails." Papa's voice was calm, but his hands moved restlessly over the surface of the desk.

Elizabeth covered her mouth to muffle her gasp. "Oh, Papa!" Tears spilled out of her eyes and ran unchecked down her cheeks.

Her father nodded slowly. "I know. I am not a young man. I had hoped for more time, but..." His hands once again worried the frame of his spectacles. "For my own sake, I have made peace with it, but I do wish you girls could be safely married." He ran his hand through the thinning hair over his forehead; many strands of gray had recently joined the strands of brown. "I had intended to father a son. And when it became clear that was not to be..." He bowed his head, showing the weight of his years. "I should have run my business affairs more carefully. That is the truth."

"Oh no, Papa!" Lizzy cried. She jumped up and hurried around the desk so she could kneel beside her father's chair. "'Tis nothing but the vagaries of fate! Our situation can scarcely be laid at your door."

"If it pleases you to say it...." Her father patted the hand she laid on his arm. "I must confess to being a coward as well. I have not shared this news with your mother. I did not wish her to worry—or shriek." Elizabeth and her father exchanged a knowing look.

Elizabeth stood, leaning against the desk for support. "Do not be anxious for our future. The solution has been presented to us just in time." She swallowed hard. "I shall marry Mr. Collins and then when you..." She noticed a tremor in her voice. "And then Mama and my sisters will not be forced to leave Longbourn. It is the perfect solution."

Her father leaned back into his chair, looking very frail. "Yes, indeed, it would be perfect if Mr. Collins were a sensible person. If he were not living proof that the Good Lord has a sense of humor. But I would not ask you to make such a sacrifice! I would have you marry for love." The corners of his lips, indeed his whole face, seemed to be dragged down by the weight of his burdens.

"You are not asking; I am offering. Yes, I had hoped for love, but I have always known the chances of finding it were never very great. I am much too outspoken, and I have little dowry. I love Longbourn and my family, so I would be marrying for a different kind of love." She attempted to catch her father's eye, but his head remained bowed.

"Perhaps Mr. Collins's affections might be transferred to one of the other girls…"

Elizabeth took her father's cold hand in hers, touched by how much he cared for her. "Mary has stated more than once in Mr. Collins's presence that she has no intention of ever marrying. Kitty and Lydia are too young and silly. And Jane… I could not ask that of her." Elizabeth wanted to believe Mr. Bingley would return for Jane, and nothing should stand in the way of her sister's happiness.

"But—"

Elizabeth formed her lips into a semblance of a smile. "My marriage will bring happiness to you and Mama and the family. And it will ensure our future. That will make me very happy indeed." Kneeling again, she tried to radiate an air of calm acceptance, although it was not one of her strengths. *Perhaps Jane can give me lessons.*

Her father placed his other hand on hers. "I must confess it would set my mind at ease to know the family future would be secured."

"It will be." Elizabeth squeezed his fingers briefly.

Papa shifted in his seat, looking at the window. "I have said nothing of my health to anyone. I think it best if it remains that way."

"Yes, of course," Elizabeth said. Even with the promise of security through her marriage to Mr. Collins, her mother would be beside herself with anxiety. "Your health might continue to be good for quite a time. No need to worry about it now."

"Yes, just as Mr. Bartlett said." He turned his gaze back to Elizabeth. Tears glistened in the corners of his eyes. "Oh, my darling girl, you have ever been a comfort to me."

She gave her father a watery smile. "And you have been my strength, Papa."

Her father discreetly wiped his eyes and straightened in his chair. Elizabeth stood.

"Now, go and give Mr. Collins the good news. It is far more than he deserves." Her father picked up his book. "I am nearly to the end of this book, and I mean to finish it today." He managed to smile at her before lowering his eyes to the book, but he blinked rapidly as he commenced reading.

Before opening the door, Elizabeth wiped her eyes with a handkerchief, wishing to avoid awkward questions about red-rimmed eyes and blotchy skin. *Although Mr. Collins would certainly interpret them as tears of joy.*

But no, she must not be bitter. She must only dwell on the good things about the marriage. This union will make her father happy, her family happy, Mr. Collins happy. Only one person would not be happy.

But that does not matter, she told herself firmly and opened the door.

Chapter 2

"I had a letter from Jane Bennet yesterday."

These words, falling from the lips of Caroline Bingley, had the power to make Darcy's gaze lurch in her direction. Was that her intent? The smirk forming on her lips suggested it might be. He turned his gaze back to the fireplace.

Darcy had invited Bingley to tea at Darcy House, and the addition of Miss Bingley to the party had been an unwelcome surprise. When she had followed her brother into the drawing room, Bingley had given Darcy a small, apologetic shrug. Darcy was most concerned about her effect on Georgiana, who found Miss Bingley intimidating. When would Bingley ever learn to gainsay his sister?

So far, however, the afternoon had proceeded smoothly. Georgiana had not uttered a word, but at least had remained in the room. Then Miss Bingley had proceeded to introduce this sensitive topic of conversation.

Charles Bingley was hardly less interested in his sister's surprise announcement than Darcy. He shifted in his chair and set down his tea cup. "Ja-Miss Bennet wrote to you? W-what news is there from Meryton?" He made no attempt to sound casual.

Enjoying the effect she had on her listeners, his sister leaned back in her chair and drawled, "They have had a good deal of rain over the past fortnight."

Bingley rolled his eyes. "Yes. And?"

"Jane's Aunt Phillips had a cold but seems to be improving." Miss Bingley's smirk only widened.

Bingley made a frustrated noise. "Is that all?"

Darcy could sympathize. Her triumphant tone suggested she had news of great import, but perhaps she was simply teasing them. Darcy settled back in his chair and took a sip of tea.

Caroline Bingley had been the only member of their party at Netherfield who had guessed about Darcy's attraction to Elizabeth. Three months before, he had left Hertfordshire determined to forget everything about Elizabeth Bennet but had found the task far more difficult than he anticipated. Elizabeth haunted his days and nights without ceasing. During the day, his thoughts turned to her: her musical laugh, teasing voice, light and pleasing figure. At night, he struggled to sleep, and when he did, he dreamed of her.

Again and again, he had examined the problem but had always determined there was no other solution than to banish her from his thoughts. So far, he had met with little success, and now this reminder from Miss Bingley only threatened to further disturb his equanimity.

Georgiana nibbled a biscuit, attempting to appear interested in a conversation about people she had never met.

"Caroline—" Bingley's voice held a note of warning.

Miss Bingley sighed dramatically as if extremely put out by her brother's demands. "Well... There was one item of interest. One of Jane's sisters is engaged to be married to that parson who is a cousin of theirs." Miss Bingley sneered, a singularly unattractive expression.

"Mr. Collins," Darcy supplied.

"Yes, that is his name."

Darcy's chest compressed with anxiety, making it hard to breathe. "Which sister?"

"The second. Elizabeth." Miss Bingley slid him a look that could not be interpreted as anything less than triumphant.

It was now *impossible* for Darcy to breathe. What had happened to the air in the room?

Elizabeth! Engaged to that idiot? Married to that fool for the rest of her life? Going to his bed? Bearing his children?

No! It was not possible. Darcy needed to protest the impossibility of this pronouncement, refute it immediately, but nothing emerged from his mouth save a strangled gurgle. Georgiana's gaze shifted to him, wide-eyed with alarm.

Bingley, fortunately, had not lost his powers of speech. "Engaged to Mr. Collins! I thought she had more sense."

"She does," Darcy growled. "There must be some error."

Miss Bingley's laugh held no actual mirth. "Jane would hardly make such a mistake!"

"The man is a fool!" Darcy expostulated. "How could she accept him?"

Georgiana had plastered herself against the back of her chair, her eyes never leaving his face. His outburst was out of character, he knew, but at the moment, he could not find the means to control himself.

"Now that I think of it," Bingley said, "I do recall that Collins danced two dances with her at the Netherfield Ball."

"Yes, he danced very ill!" Darcy said.

"Perhaps he had been courting her back then," Bingley concluded.

Darcy closed his eyes and considered this. The idiot parson had danced with Elizabeth and made a fool of himself. He had tried to engage her in conversation, but Darcy had seen no signs of interest on her part. Elizabeth had far too much sense. She had been mortified when Collins had presumed to converse with Darcy without an introduction. No, it was impossible. How could she have accepted his hand?

When he opened his eyes, he noticed the gaze of everyone in the room upon him. Damnation! He too easily betrayed himself when it came to Elizabeth Bennet!

Taking a bite of a biscuit he had no interest in, Darcy attempted to appear more casual. "Did Miss Bennet's letter say when the wedding is to take place?" he asked, taking a sip of tea and attempting to calm the trembling in his hands.

"No." Miss Bingley's tone was sharp.

Good Lord! They could already be wed! This thought constricted his throat, and he almost choked as he swallowed his biscuit.

"Miss Bennet did tell me that Longbourn is entailed away from the female line," Bingley said. "Mr. Collins will inherit it upon Mr. Bennet's death."

Blast! Why had he not known that Longbourn was entailed? It was a common enough practice. He should have thought to inquire. "I did not know," Darcy murmured, now feeling faintly nauseous.

Mr. Collins must have resolved to choose a wife from among his cousins since he was to inherit their home. And he did not select Jane because everyone believed she would marry Bingley....

Elizabeth would have accepted his offer for the good of her family. He had not misjudged her powers of discernment after all. She recognized the man's stupidity but sacrificed her future happiness—all her future happiness—so her family would not have to leave their ancestral home.

For a moment Darcy feared he might be sick. She would be married forever to man she could not love—or even respect. *What a horrible fate.*

"So she accepted the proposal for the sake of her family?" Georgiana entered the conversation for the first time. Clearly Elizabeth's dilemma had drawn his sister's compassion. *At least Georgiana would never need to make such an awful choice*, Darcy thought warmly. *Far better she died an old maid than marry such a man.*

Bingley nodded. "Yes, I believe so."

"What a sacrifice to make!" Georgiana exclaimed. "She must be an exceptional woman."

Miss Bingley's expression turned from triumphant to sour.

"She is indeed," Darcy agreed while simultaneously wishing she were more selfish and less devoted to her family.

And now she is lost to me. Before I ever had her. My Elizabeth is gone.

***

The Bingleys had departed. Georgiana had bid him goodnight long ago, but Darcy had not retired to his bedchamber. Sleep would be impossible. For hours, he paced in his study: door to fireplace, desk to sideboard. Again and again until his feet were sore from walking and his shoulders ached with tension. But he could not stop. He even considered removing to the downstairs hallway or the drawing room where he could pace more freely. However, a servant might be awake, and he had no wish to explain himself.

How could he explain it to another when he barely understood it himself?

Darcy took another sip from his crystal glass. He had carefully measured out the brandy. Although being foxed held immense appeal to him, this situation required a clear head.

With Miss Bingley's news, any small success he had achieved in his endeavors to forget Elizabeth had been utterly shattered. More than ever before, Elizabeth once again occupied his mind and pulled at his soul until his every thought was filled with images of her face and the sound of her voice—and the anguish of knowing he had lost her.

Over and over throughout the evening, he had ordered himself to forget her. She was engaged to another man and no longer his concern. In fact, she had never been his concern even when she had been free to accept his hand.

The reasons he could not marry Elizabeth were still valid. They were serious and plentiful. Nothing about her family's situation had changed. Yet now he wished desperately he had ignored his misgivings in November and made her an offer.

Darcy sank into a chair; for a moment, he indulged his imagination with this fantasy. If he had proposed, she would now be Mrs. Darcy and safe from Mr. Collins. And she would be waiting for him upstairs in the chambers for the mistress of the house. With her dark hair spread over the pillow and her fine, sparkling eyes watching him, filled with desire…

The image filled him with a golden glow as warmth spread throughout his body.

Unbidden, the vision transformed into one of Elizabeth lying in a cold, hard bed, stoically awaiting her wedding night with Collins.

"No!" Darcy hurled the glass at the fireplace where it shattered on the hearth. If he could not change this future, he must not allow himself to surrender to such visions.

Instead, he must forget Elizabeth Bennet. Yes, surely with time, his emotions would fade, and he would forget her. Their paths were unlikely to cross again.

Except that damnable man was his aunt's parson. Whenever Darcy went to Rosings, there would be Collins—and Elizabeth. Wearing the white cap of a married woman and a dreary, sensible gown. Listening obediently to her idiotic husband while the liveliness and independence seeped out of her face with every passing year. And her body growing heavy with his child...

"Damnation!" Darcy slumped into a chair, pressing his hands to his eyes, wishing he could wash such images from his mind. It was not to be borne!

He would avoid visiting Rosings. And maybe all of Kent. And Hertfordshire. And London, in case the Collinses visited the city.

Perhaps he would become a recluse at Pemberley.

Darcy slumped even further into the chair. If only she were marrying someone else...anyone other than that toadying man. If she were betrothed to some country squire, at least he could believe she might love him.

No, Darcy would still loathe the man.

But Collins...

Tonight, Darcy hated the stupid parson with a white-hot passion.

Darcy stood and strode to the sideboard. Perhaps getting foxed had something to recommend it. He grabbed a new glass and the decanter. Amber liquid splashed into the fine crystal. All of this luxury, this fortune, and he could not have the one thing he truly desired: the first woman who had truly interested him after all these years. The *only* woman who made his heart flip like a performing dog.

Darcy stopped with the glass halfway to his lips.

Elizabeth was the first woman who had ever captivated him like this. He had not seen her for months, and still he could recall in great detail every expression on her face, every nuance in her voice.

"No," he insisted. "There will be other women." He raised the glass again.

Then stopped.

"I am eight and twenty." It bore repeating. He had been meeting young women for years. Dozens of women. Hundreds. It was safe to say he had met most of the women the ton had to offer, and he did not care for any of them. Many were pretty or somewhat diverting, but none had affected him like Elizabeth. When he was with her, his whole being was alive. He did not understand it at all, but somehow she awakened his soul.

How could he do without her for the rest of his life? Bracing his hands on the sideboard, he hung his head.

When he thought of her, the rest of the world fell away.

When he thought of marriage, there was Elizabeth—and then there were all the other women in the world. Finally, Darcy gulped his brandy, savoring the burn in his throat. If only he had stayed in Hertfordshire! Perhaps he could have prevented Collins's proposal.

Somehow.

No, even in Meryton he could have accomplished little…short of proposing to Elizabeth himself. Wealth afforded him some privileges, but they did not extend to preventing unrelated women from accepting other men's proposals.

And now it was too late. Yes, she was not officially wed, but a betrothal was tantamount to a marriage. The marriage contracts had undoubtedly been signed and announcements placed in the paper.

Unless…

An idea began to take shape in Darcy's mind. Men almost never broke engagements; their honor was at stake. Darcy snorted aloud at the thought that Collins concerned himself with his personal honor.

However, women occasionally did break engagements. Yes, it was somewhat scandalous, but a scandal would be forgotten with time.

Elizabeth naturally had harbored no hopes that Darcy might propose. The barriers between them would seem insurmountable to her, particularly since she was likely unaware of the depth of his partiality for her. But if

Darcy had made her an offer, she undoubtedly would have chosen him.

If she were presented with another choice—someone who could care for her family as well as, or better than, her cousin—she might be persuaded to end the engagement. No, it was certain; she would be persuaded to end it! Despite the small scandal, Darcy had far more to offer than Collins; she would be delighted at the offer.

Darcy shifted uneasily in his seat. It was not a precisely honorable goal: to break another man's engagement. But to prevent great sorrow for Elizabeth, he was willing to sacrifice much, even honor.

Yes, such a step was necessary, not only for his happiness but also for Elizabeth's. He would be rescuing her from a lifetime of misery.

Darcy resumed pacing with an energy that could not be contained. A plan took shape in his mind. He would ride to Longbourn, court Elizabeth surreptitiously, and persuade her to accept him.

Abruptly Darcy stopped in his tracks. Would he really do this? After months of trying to forget Elizabeth, how had he so abruptly made the decision to propose?

But he must own the truth. After months of denying his feelings, he found the reasons to object to their union dissolved like sugar in tea. The prospect of losing Elizabeth had shown him how specious these obstacles had always been.

Proposing to Elizabeth was the right course; he felt this certainty in the core of his being. Yes, he would travel to Hertfordshire in the morning. He would rescue Elizabeth, and in the process—he now realized—rescue himself from a lifetime of loneliness.

***

Bingley had been happy to lend Darcy the use of Netherfield for the duration of his visit, although he had been surprised to learn of his friend's sudden, unseasonable desire to hunt grouse. As soon as Darcy's trunk had been unloaded from the carriage, he had borrowed a horse from Bingley's stable and taken the road to Longbourn.

Halfway to Longbourn, he spied a familiar person descending the path from Oakham Mount. Her figure was light and pleasing as always, but what first caught his eye was the way Elizabeth moved. The grace of her step and the ease of her movement had apparently indelibly tattooed themselves on his memory. Darcy experienced a moment of cold fear at the thought he might fail in his mission. He did not know how he would survive. But he immediately banished such thoughts. How could he possibly fail?

Darcy dismounted from his horse at the place where the path met the road—and tied the reins to a nearby branch. As she reached him, Elizabeth's eyes widened in recognition and surprise, but her smile was brief and shallow. Did she quicken her step? He could not discern.

Finally, she was within speaking distance. "Miss Bennet." He gave her a short bow.

"Mr. Darcy." She made a small curtsey. "I am astonished to see you here. How long have you been in the neighborhood?"

"I only arrived today. I had a sudden urge to do some hunting." Darcy knew this was a weak excuse for visiting Hertfordshire. It was hardly a popular season for hunting, and he could easily have gone to shoot at Pemberley, but it was the best excuse he had discovered. He planned to make good on the falsehood by venturing out one day and pointing a shotgun in the direction of some birds.

"Are you staying at Netherfield?" Her expression was distant and polite. He had hoped for a warmer reception, but perhaps she felt compelled to be reserved around men other than her fiancé.

"Yes, although Mr. Bingley and his sisters were unable to accompany me."

"Oh." Elizabeth quickly hid her disappointment. *She must still have hopes of Bingley and her sister, for I cannot believe she misses Miss Bingley and Mrs. Hurst!*

"I hope you left them in good health?" she asked.

"Yes, they all are in excellent health."

The conversation stuttered to a stop. As Elizabeth regarded him, a crease formed between her eyebrows as if he were a mystery she needed to solve. Darcy fully felt the awkwardness of his sudden arrival; he was not, after all, well acquainted with her family.

"I hope your family is in good health?" he asked.

"Yes, everyone is enjoying very good health."

Silence stretched out between them. Elizabeth's eyes darted in the direction of Longbourn as if she were wishing to be on her way.

The wan early April sunshine provided the opportunity to examine Elizabeth in more detail. Despite her slim figure, she appeared to have lost weight since he had last seen her. Dark shadows haunted her eyes. *She does not appear to be a happy future bride.*

He stifled a completely inappropriate impulse to pull her into his arms with a promise to comfort and protect her for the rest of her life. He wanted to chase those shadows from her eyes and help her gain weight, even if it meant feeding her by hand—a thought that held alarming appeal.

Elizabeth shifted her position, drawing his attention to their awkward silence. "I was on my way to Longbourn to pay my respects to your family," Darcy said. "If you are venturing in that direction, perhaps I may accompany you?"

Elizabeth blinked rapidly. "You were coming to visit Longbourn?"

Why did she sound so incredulous? "Well…yes. I am not well acquainted with many of the other families in the neighborhood."

A ghost of her pert smile appeared on her lips. "I would not think you inclined to socialize at all. Did you not find country society confined and unvarying?"

Oh, Good Lord! Had he said that? His anxiety in Elizabeth's presence had undoubtedly caused him to say many foolish things the previous autumn. If only he could go back in time and slap himself!

"It is true that one might not find as great a variety of people here as in the city, but I find myself growing weary of the society in London as well." Perhaps such a statement might mitigate any lingering bad feelings he had engendered.

"I would imagine so." The smile was gone, in favor of a more contemplative look. Darcy wished he might provoke the expression again.

"May I accompany you to Longbourn?" he asked.

Elizabeth's voice was all politeness, but she did not smile. "Of course. Everyone will be very surprised to see you!"

And hopefully pleased, Darcy thought. However, Elizabeth's welcome was not as warm as he might have hoped. Perhaps she felt distressed to see him when she was now betrothed to another. Darcy took his horse's reins, and the beast followed them as they walked down the lane.

Despite his unease, Darcy noticed how the exercise brought out the color in Elizabeth's complexion. Her cheeks were a delicate rosy hue, and her eyes were shining brightly in the afternoon sunshine. If only he could reach out and touch her cheek! Would her skin be as soft as he imagined? If only he could stroke one of those delicate curls. He could easily imagine the silky texture under his fingertips.

Darcy averted his eyes and attempted to turn his thoughts to safer subjects. However, neither his body nor his mind seemed inclined to obey his better judgment. He might as well surrender to his desires and imagine taking her to bed. His whole body responded to that thought; Darcy suppressed a groan.

Elizabeth looked at him oddly. Had he made a noise? *Good God! Not yet five minutes in her company and already I am making a fool of myself! Say something!* "Ah…you are looking particularly well today, Miss Elizabeth," he said. "Quite lovely."

She gave him a blank stare. Did she not expect compliments from him? Then her lips twisted in an ironic smile. "I thought you found me tolerable, but not pretty enough to tempt you."

What? "I beg your pardon?"

Elizabeth's eyes were fixed on the road ahead. "At the Meryton Assembly, it was the reason you gave for declining to dance with me when Mr. Bingley suggested it."

"Who told you I said that?" he demanded.

"No one. I overheard you." The tone of her voice was cool, but she had to be angry.

Good Lord! Darcy rubbed his jaw. All he remembered from that evening was irritation at Bingley for dragging them to the provincial hell and annoyance that Bingley's sister would not cease importuning him. Being in a foul mood, he might have said something cutting, but he did not recall voicing an opinion about Elizabeth. Now he wished he could go back in time and shoot himself. It would save a lot of trouble.

"I-I must apologize. I was in a particularly ill humor that evening, or I would not have said something so patently false. I beg you to accept my apology." Sweat dampened his collar and the front of his shirt. He tugged at his cravat where it seemed to be choking him.

Elizabeth turned her head to regard him, eyebrows raised in surprise. Had she believed him incapable of apologizing? But her eyes turned back to the road before he could decipher her expression. "Of course. It is of no matter." Her voice was still frustratingly indifferent. Darcy would have preferred her to yell at him.

Damnation! *Does she believe I am lying now and only seek to flatter her vanity?* It would be a bitter irony, indeed, that the most beautiful woman of his acquaintance would think he only tolerated her.

Silence had prevailed for a minute or more; Darcy needed to say something. "I do find you quite lovely."

Elizabeth's gaze turned on him, one eyebrow raised. *Blast! She does not understand me at all.* "Believe me, I do not indulge in idle flattery." Oh, he was making a hash of this! She would believe him incapable of conducting a simple conversation with a woman.

And she would be quite correct.

Elizabeth tugged her pelisse so it covered more of her bodice. The early spring days were still quite cool. "You have now determined I am handsome enough to tempt you?"

The words hung in the air between them, suggesting meanings Darcy was certain Elizabeth had not intended.

"That is—I mean—" She blushed quite becomingly. "You would be tempted to *dance* with me now?"

"Indeed," Darcy responded quickly. "If you recall, I asked you to dance at the Netherfield ball."

"Yes, I remember." Her voice was soft. Was it a good memory for her?

Darcy brushed road dust from his breeches, unable to think of something else to say. He had anticipated that seeing Elizabeth once more would be awkward, but not quite so awkward. If she indeed believed he held her in such low esteem, perhaps she had not perceived his later admiration of her. That would make his task more difficult than he anticipated.

"We have been enjoying unusually fine weather," Elizabeth said after several minutes of silence. They engaged in a discussion about the weather and the latest happenings in Meryton. But Elizabeth's conversation lacked its usual animation, and Darcy cursed himself for having created the awkwardness between them.

Elizabeth said nothing of her engagement, and Darcy felt uneasy about raising the topic. She could not have any suspicion that he had arrived with the intention of separating her from Collins. It was unlikely that she suspected he could overcome his reservations about her family.

The stilted conversation ended when they arrived at Longbourn. The Bennets' housekeeper took Darcy's hat and coat, and Elizabeth escorted him to the drawing room, explaining that they had not expected visitors and that she would alert her mother to his presence.

He braced himself accordingly.

Darcy sat, alone, in the drawing room for a minute or more. A maid entered, set a tea service on the table, and hastily exited. Darcy realized she had left the door ajar, creating a cool draft from the hallway. He stood to close the door but stopped when he heard voices from out in the hall.

"Lord! Mr. Darcy is here? Whatever does he want? He is as dull as one of Mary's books of sermons!"

Darcy grimaced, but fought against any impulse to take offense. The voice belonged to one of the youngest Bennet sisters, Lydia or… He could not recall the other girl's name. They were silly girls. Let them think him dull.

"Lydia, he is our guest, and we must be polite to him." The gentle voice belonged to Elizabeth's oldest sister, Jane.

Lydia sighed dramatically. "I cannot imagine why he has come. He just sits and scowls." Darcy was not pleased to hear this assessment of his demeanor, but Lydia was hardly the best judge of character.

He heard Elizabeth's voice for the first time. "I know, Lydia! I cannot say why he graced us with his presence since he dislikes us so much and disapproves of our family. I was hoping for news of Mr. Bingley, but he has not hinted at it." *Good Lord! Is this Elizabeth's opinion of me?* Darcy experienced a momentary impulse to flee the drawing room before anyone arrived—and take a fast horse back to London.

"Perhaps his opinion has improved over time," Jane suggested. Darcy was warming to her.

"No, I am certain I do not have his good opinion, and if I do, he has bestowed it most unwillingly. We all know him to be a proud, difficult man." Elizabeth's voice shook with vehemence. Darcy's stomach knotted more tightly, making him feel slightly nauseous.

"Lizzy!" Jane admonished. "You—"

"Girls! Here I come!" Mrs. Bennet's voice was accompanied by the taps of her heels on the stairs.

Darcy hastily closed the door and retreated to a chair near the window where he tried to relax his shoulders and smooth his face out of a grimace. When his hostesses arrived, he did not want to show them the surly, difficult man they believed him to be. He should not have eavesdropped, and now he was paying for his sins.

However, the realization of Elizabeth's true opinion tilted his world on its axis. Only now did he realize how little thought he had given to the question of her feelings for him. He had perceived her as flirting with him, enjoying his attentions, and hoping for his regard. But what if she had not? Had he simply made assumptions about affection that never existed?

He tasted bitter irony. All his life, he had sought to avoid fortune hunters, yet he had expected Elizabeth to fall into his arms because of that fortune.

He had believed that she would eagerly accept an offer should he make one. He thought she knew of his regard and would be delighted to learn he could overlook the obstacles presented by her family. But now…now he knew her opinion of him was so low that if she accepted his offer, it would only be for reasons of financial security.

Like Collins.

In fact, the primary quality that set him apart from Collins was that he had far more fortune to offer. But Elizabeth would be no happier accepting his proposal than she was accepting one from Collins.

Darcy reconsidered his desire to bolt out of the door. Or perhaps the window would open wide enough…

The door swung open, and Mrs. Bennet sailed in, followed by the three daughters he had heard conversing in the hallway. He stood to bow, and the ladies made him a perfunctory curtsey. "Mr. Darcy, you are welcome to our home." Mrs. Bennet's tone belied her words. Her formal manner had none of the warmth or excessive solicitousness she had displayed toward Bingley.

He had expected her to welcome him joyfully, at least because she hoped he would marry one of her daughters. But apparently, he was too proud and difficult even for her. What a lowering thought. They all sat, and Elizabeth poured out tea for everyone.

Different emotions washed over Darcy as the conversation moved from weather (mild) to happenings in the neighborhood (boring) to fashion (very boring) to the activities of the Bingleys (awkward). However, the conversation occupied only half his attention while the other half was mired in agitation.

His momentary rush of anger at Elizabeth for her harsh words had been followed by self-recriminations. What had she said that he did not deserve? Dark despair quickly followed. If she disliked him so much, she might not even consider him an acceptable alternative to Collins.

It was a particularly galling thought.

How could she prefer a lifetime of misery with that obsequious toad to the joy he could bring her as mistress of Pemberley?

Perhaps she does not deserve me if she is so short-sighted, a voice whispered at the back of his mind. But he thought her opinion might be based on misimpressions, and he was seized with the need to correct them.

However, the task simply seemed daunting. Not only would he need to convince her to abandon her existing engagement, but he also would need to greatly improve himself in her estimation.

"—Mr. Collins!"

Darcy had not been attending to Mrs. Bennet's overly abundant conversation and had, therefore, missed an important turn in the subject. Damnation! What had she said?

Darcy took a sip of tea and inspected the other faces for a clue about the topic, but their expressions revealed nothing. "Mr. Collins? Indeed?" Hopefully the response made some sense.

Mrs. Bennet settled back on her settee with a self-satisfied air. "Yes, he made Lizzy an offer a few days after you left for London. He has the living at Hunsford Parsonage, and his patroness is Lady Catherine de Bourgh! According to Mr. Collins, she has a grand house and very fine manners."

Darcy managed, barely, not to choke on his tea.

Elizabeth's face was quite red. "Mama, Mr. Darcy is Lady Catherine's nephew."

"Are you?" Mrs. Bennet's voice rose an octave. "Well, then you know how grand her house is." Darcy finally received a smile from her—for entirely the wrong reason.

"Yes, it is very big," he agreed. Elizabeth, clearly mortified by her mother's effusions, kept her eyes fixed on the hands folded in her lap. Seeking a way to divert the conversation, Darcy said the first thing that came to him. "When will you go into Kent, Miss Elizabeth?"

He cursed this impulse when her face went from red to white in a matter of seconds. "In about a month." Her face was still, bearing no resemblance to a happy bride.

"Mr. Collins wanted it to be sooner, but Mama needed more time to do the wedding clothes and the trousseau!" Lydia blurted out. Jane sent her a quelling look, but Lydia ignored her older sister.

"Yes, there is a vast deal to be done when preparing for a wedding!" Mrs. Bennet exclaimed. "The first of my daughters to be married! You are so fortunate to be singled out by Mr. Collins!"

Elizabeth made no reply. Her eyes were downcast, and a touch of wetness sparkled on her cheek.

"Lizzy!" Mrs. Bennet demanded a response, and Darcy fought a most ungentlemanlike impulse to shout at her.

"Lizzy is a little sad to be leaving Longbourn," Jane chimed in.

Mrs. Bennet fussed with the shawl about her shoulders. "Well, naturally she is. But that is the way of things. Women must leave home and live with their husbands."

Despite his irritation with Elizabeth's mother, Darcy was struck by the truth in her words. He had always known he would live at Pemberley all his life, but Elizabeth and her sisters had expected to be forced to leave their childhood home. Indeed, women's lives required a particular kind of bravery.

But in this situation, Mrs. Bennet might misinterpreting the true source of Elizabeth's distress. If she were happy about marrying Collins, she could undoubtedly bear the loss of Longbourn well enough. At least Darcy hoped this was the situation; Pemberley was quite a bit further than Hunsford.

He could not draw his eyes away from the sight of her tear-stained face. He hated watching his Elizabeth in such anguish.

His Elizabeth?

This was the woman who had provoked his anger and despair with her words in the hallway minutes earlier. And yet now he still felt only compassion…anguish…love.

In fact, his love for her had not been diminished one bit.

He had arrived in Hertfordshire for the purpose of making Elizabeth happy. Despite everything, he was still committed to that course. The woman he loved was miserable, and he must find a way to help her.

What if such help did not entail marrying him? Darcy's heart quailed at the thought. Could he free her from Collins and let her go?

His thoughts refused to pursue that path. She disliked him because she did not know him. He would improve her opinion of him; he must believe that or surrender to despair.

He would show her his true nature. Impress her with his good manners and fine understanding. And he must somehow find a way to break her engagement— without causing a scandal.

Darcy sighed. Perhaps for an encore, he could defeat Napoleon's army single-handedly.

Chapter 3

Elizabeth did not understand why Mr. Darcy was sitting in her family's drawing room.

This was the third day since his return to Hertfordshire, and he had visited every afternoon. Mrs. Bennet had insisted that Elizabeth sit with the man since she had a prior acquaintance with him; however, her mother's nerves prevented her from attending to their proud and troublesome guest. Kitty and Lydia moaned and complained if they were asked entertain him. Mary did not complain but would say almost nothing to him. Only Jane would accompany Elizabeth to the drawing room, and for that favor, she was eternally grateful.

Mr. Darcy's visits were characterized by bursts of stilted conversation followed by periods of awkward silence. Occasionally, Elizabeth and Mr. Darcy would happen upon a book or piece of music they both appreciated, and a lively conversation would follow. Even when they disagreed, their debates were spirited and enjoyable. His eyes would shine during such dialogues, and his whole face would be alive with animation. At such times, Elizabeth was sharply reminded of the kind of companionship she would never enjoy in Mr. Collins's presence.

But these events were far too rare for Elizabeth to experience Mr. Darcy's visits as relaxed and pleasant. Too often, he would simply watch Jane and Elizabeth converse with each other. Or they would sit in a strained silence. Sometimes, Elizabeth glanced up from her needlework to discover his eyes fixed on her. Did he so disapprove of her behavior that he needed to stare at her? It was unsettling. He did not observe Jane in the same way. Was he intent on cataloguing her missteps and faux pas so he could laugh at them with his friends upon his return to London? Such thoughts made her even more self-conscious under the force of his gaze.

Why did he insist on visiting Longbourn? Why could he not take his disapproving looks and proud mien to visit Lucas Lodge?

She considered the possibility that he wished to discern Jane's feelings for Bingley, but he made few attempts to talk with Jane and rarely mentioned his friend. On the other hand, if his purpose was mostly to disapprove of her family and congratulate himself on his superior manners, he had gone to quite a bit of trouble.

Sometimes Mr. Darcy would ask her to play the pianoforte and sing, although she knew not why. She could only display her lack of talent; certainly, his sister must be far more accomplished. However, he was an appreciative listener, and she enjoyed performing for him. At such moments of weakness, she chastised herself for enjoying the company of the man who had ruined Wickham's life and would resolve again to be quiet and sullen in his presence.

Somehow, despite Mr. Darcy's unpleasantness, she was finding this vow hard to keep.

Upon occasion, he would ask her odd questions about how she felt to be leaving Longbourn or how often she planned to visit Hertfordshire. Not wishing to dwell on her upcoming nuptials, she always attempted to change the topic.

On the rare occasions when Elizabeth's mother visited the drawing room, Mr. Darcy was polite—the model of gentlemanly behavior. Unfortunately, her mother was still predisposed against him and did not recognize his attempts to be civil. Elizabeth found herself regretting how freely she had spread her opinions of Mr. Darcy in the autumn.

Today, Elizabeth was in an even greater state of agitation, for Mr. Collins was expected. This would be her fiancé's first visit since the proposal, and she was not anticipating it with pleasure. She had managed to persuade him to a long engagement without a definite wedding date. However, he would, of course, broach the subject of the wedding and her removal to Kent—two events she wished to forget.

Facing her fiancé in Mr. Darcy's presence would be an added burden. She did not know how Mr. Collins would make a fool of himself, but she knew he would—by fawning over Mr. Darcy perhaps, or by extolling Rosings Park as if it were the Garden of Eden.

It had been mortifying enough when Mr. Darcy had aimed a haughty stare at Mr. Collins when he was merely her cousin, but now that he was her fiancé...

What must he think of her, tying herself to such a stupid man for the rest of her life? Even if he knew about the entail, he would only believe she was a slave to mercenary considerations.

Oh, if only Mr. Darcy would go and shoot some birds!

Elizabeth attempted to drag her attention back to the conversation in the room. Mr. Darcy had mentioned recent battles on the Peninsula and seemed surprised that Elizabeth and Jane were knowledgeable about them. He had engaged in quite an interesting account of a recent battle from the perspective of his cousin, a colonel who had fought. Surprisingly, he was quite a good storyteller. Every word displayed his love and admiration for his cousin. Not for the first time, Elizabeth doubted the accuracy of Mr. Wickham's account of Mr. Darcy's character.

Elizabeth was laughing at a repetition of the cousin's witticisms when Hill entered the drawing room to announce Mr. Collins. Elizabeth's laughter immediately died. *Here will be the end to all intelligent conversation.*

Then she felt guilty. *No, I should not have such uncharitable thoughts about my betrothed.*

Setting aside her needlework, Mrs. Bennet arose and greeted Mr. Collins with an excessive enthusiasm she had never displayed toward Mr. Darcy. Mr. Collins rushed across the room to Elizabeth and latched onto her hand. "My darling! It has been so long since our parting!" The very loudness and effusiveness of his gestures meant they would have been appropriate for the London stage. Mr. Collins rubbed the back of her hand against his cheek in what he must have imagined was an affectionate gesture, but Elizabeth only noticed the roughness of his beard stubble.

Over Mr. Collins's shoulder, she saw Mr. Darcy glaring at the man's back. Did he disapprove of the familiarity of their greeting? "Mr. Collins," Elizabeth murmured, knowing her cheeks were turning red.

"No, Elizabeth. Your modesty does you credit, but you must call me by my given name. For we are soon to know each other on a most *intimate* basis." His smile might have been intended to convey affection, but it emerged as a leer.

Elizabeth's stomach churned. She cast her eyes down, unwilling to meet the gaze of anyone in the room. Bad enough that her fiancé was trafficking in innuendos, but to do so before Mr. Darcy!

If only something would happen to distract everyone's attention. Lydia rushing in with news about officers and dances. Her mother's attack of the vapors. Oh, where was a plague of locusts when one needed it?

Mr. Collins turned to greet Jane and became aware of Mr. Darcy's presence. "Mr. Darcy! I did not know you were here, sir!" He bowed so deeply he almost toppled over and needed to grab a chair for support. "I pray you understand I did not intend any slight."

"No, no, of course not." Mr. Darcy frowned, almost as if he harbored some sort of resentment against the parson, but most likely, he was simply annoyed at the man's obsequious behavior.

Mr. Collins's face brightened as if he were about to impart the most wonderful secret. "I have come directly from Kent. Your aunt and cousin have been enjoying wonderful health!"

"That is good to hear," Darcy muttered.

"I do believe Miss de Bourgh's coughing has grown less frequent and less forceful than previously. And she has had more color in her cheeks these past weeks. I told her at dinner the other night, 'Miss de Bourgh, you are like a delicate English rose!'" Mr. Collins drew himself up to his full height. "I flatter myself she was well pleased with the compliment."

"I am sure." A fly in Mr. Darcy's soup could not have received a colder welcome. Mr. Collins nodded enthusiastically, completely oblivious to Mr. Darcy's tone.

Mr. Collins wasted no time in positioning himself next to Elizabeth on the loveseat, far closer than she would have liked. Mr. Darcy was scowling again. Did he disapprove of their closeness? Well, it was no matter. Betrothed couples were allowed some liberties, after all.

"Lady Catherine has been most condescendingly helpful in preparing the parsonage for my dear Elizabeth's arrival. She suggested new curtains in the upstairs sitting room and shelves in the bedchamber's closet! Is that not a capital idea?"

"A masterstroke," Darcy agreed, his face carefully neutral.

Mr. Collins took Elizabeth's hand and held it in the crook of his arm, against his body. She keenly felt the impropriety of this position, but removing her hand would only draw more attention to his actions. Was this how the rest of her life would be?

Mr. Collins patted her hand. "My dearest Elizabeth and I seem to have been formed for each other."

Mr. Darcy's walking stick clattered to the floor. "Pardon me." The man bent to retrieve it, his face an unusual shade of red. Could dropping his walking stick have cause so much embarrassment?

Undeterred, Mr. Collins gazed down on Elizabeth fondly. "We are in perfect accord in all things."

Elizabeth began to suspect Mr. Collins of knowing a completely different Elizabeth, one made of whole cloth from his imagination. Suppressing a keen urge to roll her eyes, she could do nothing but smile wanly at him.

"How fortunate." There was an odd tone in Mr. Darcy's voice that Elizabeth could not identify. She would understand if such a declaration had provoked stifled laughter or disbelief, but Mr. Darcy seemed almost— angry? No, she must be imagining it. If Mr. Collins irritated him too much, Mr. Darcy would simply leave for Netherfield—which would solve one of Elizabeth's problems for the day. Elizabeth found herself silently encouraging Mr. Collins.

He remained oblivious to Mr. Darcy's tone. "I cannot wait until that day when she will make me the happiest of men, and we can begin our lives of wedded bliss." Quickly bringing a handkerchief up to her mouth, Elizabeth pretended a cough to hide her smile. Why did he insist on speaking like a heroine in a lurid popular novel?

"But the greatest joy will be when we return to Hunsford. For, my dear," he gave her hand another clumsy pat, "Lady Catherine has promised to visit you upon your arrival! What an honor! What condescension!"

"That is very good of her!" Mrs. Bennet cried. "You are very fortunate in your situation."

"I am indeed," Mr. Collins replied. "The most fortunate man alive!" A smug smile appeared on his face.

A fit of coughing drew everyone's attention to Mr. Darcy. "My apologies, I inhaled some tea," he said when once again capable of speech. Elizabeth frowned; she would have sworn the man's tea cup had been empty for twenty minutes.

Mrs. Bennet's curt nod suggested her grudging forgiveness for interrupting a tender moment between Elizabeth and her betrothed.

Recognizing the appreciative audience he had in Mrs. Bennet, Mr. Collins continued directing his conversation to her. "Have I told you about the windows at Rosings?" He proceeded without awaiting a reply. "There are eighteen windows on the front of the house. The glazing of each cost fifty pounds! Can you imagine?" He turned his smarmy smile on Mr. Darcy. "I have heard that your estate at Pemberley is very grand. How many windows do you have at the front?"

The other man's gaze could not have been colder. "I have never counted."

Mr. Collins continued on, blithely unaware of Mr. Darcy's contempt. "I am sure they are very grand as well."

Tension rolled off Mr. Darcy like water rushing down a mountain. Clearly, Mr. Collins irritated him almost beyond endurance. Why would Mr. Darcy not return to Netherfield? He had been at Longbourn long enough. Excessively long, in fact.

"And the draperies in her large drawing room!" Mr. Collins exclaimed. "Silk imported directly from China. One hundred and fifteen yards of the finest silk!"

Mrs. Bennet gasped at the extravagance.

"I would imagine it would make an excellent topic for your next sermon," Mr. Darcy remarked dryly. "Perhaps the transience of worldly goods?"

Mr. Collins's mouth opened, and he blinked at Mr. Darcy.

Between Mr. Collins and Mr. Darcy, Elizabeth could not stand another minute in the room. She rushed to her feet. "Mr. Collins, will you join me in a turn about the garden?"

Mr. Collins looked out the window at the mostly bare branches and the wind-tossed trees, no doubt considering the cool temperatures. "W-why, certainly, my dear. I will have you to keep me warm." He turned a lascivious grin on her.

The thought made her skin crawl, and Elizabeth instantly resolved against being alone with her fiancé. She anticipated that Mr. Darcy would take this opportunity to escape the parson's inane chatter, but politeness required an invitation. "Would you care to join us?"

"Some fresh air would be welcome, thank you." Mr. Darcy stood.

Elizabeth stared stupidly at him for a moment. Why had he chosen to join them when he so obviously loathed Mr. Collins? What a troublesome man!

But there was nothing for it. Elizabeth gave Mr. Darcy a polite nod and made her way to the door. At least she would not be alone with Mr. Collins. What a wretched thought to have about one's fiancé!

Jane offered to accompany them, but Elizabeth bade her sister stay inside since she was recovering from a cold. Instead, Elizabeth put on her cloak and gloves and ventured outside with the two men.

***

Collins captured his fiancée's hand on his arm and almost dragged her along the garden pathway. Trailing behind, Darcy slowed his gait so the others would outpace him.

The parson's voice drifted on the air. "Quite a lovely garden. It reminds me of a little garden on the west side of Rosings, although of course, this one is much smaller. Lady Catherine is a proficient horticulturalist and has designed and maintained one of the finest gardens in England. Unfortunately her gout prevents her from venturing outside frequently, but as Lady Catherine herself says, 'One may learn much about a garden just by viewing it through the window...'"

Belatedly, Darcy realized the pain in his jaw was caused by grinding his teeth together. For the sake of his molars, he needed to put distance between himself and Collins's soliloquy. Lingering near the house, Darcy pretended fascination with a rather scrawny boxwood hedge.

Simply watching Elizabeth walking with Collins provoked violent thoughts in Darcy's imagination. He might have been capable of ceding her to another man, someone he respected. But this imbecile...no, it was insupportable.

A sharp shiver traveled up his spine. Although the day was fairly mild, Darcy buttoned up his coat to ward off the occasional cool breezes. With Elizabeth on his arm, Collins seemed quite relaxed and warm, curse him.

Now the other man was making grand, dramatic gestures—no doubt accompanying some equally grand declarations. Collins's extravagant pronouncements of devotion to Elizabeth had the opposite of their intended effect. The more Collins proclaimed, the less Darcy believed him. His words could apply to any woman.

Collins knew nothing of Elizabeth's interests or passions and saw no value in her fascinating conversation or pert opinions. And he showed no inclination to learn anything about her. He declaimed his love for her as if he were reading lines from a script—for a particularly horrible, cliché-ridden play. Elizabeth herself was interchangeable with any other unattached woman of appropriate age and station.

Did that made Darcy more or less angry? On the one hand, he was relieved that no real feeling existed between the two, but on the other, he was disgusted that Collins had no understanding of his good fortune in securing the hand of such a woman.

At that moment, he would give anything to change places with his aunt's parson. *What a strange world I inhabit.*

Collins still held Elizabeth's hand captive on his arm despite her obvious discomfort. Darcy's whole body grew stiff and hot with anger, surging with the desire to forcibly remove Collins from her side—perhaps with hands around his neck to make the removal permanent. Darcy's fingers flexed eagerly at the thought. Patiently, he reminded himself why homicide would be a bad idea.

Collins was droning on about Lady Catherine's plans for the garden at Hunsford Parsonage. Elizabeth's eyes met Darcy's, and she quickly glanced away. The night of his arrival, Darcy had been dispirited by what he had learned and considered simply returning to London, but he found he could not give up the slim hope that he could yet win her heart. He did not fool himself now that he had made great progress in substantially altering Elizabeth's opinion of him, but at least she seemed happier in his presence than with Collins. It was a small victory, but he would celebrate it.

Thus, it was all the more painful to picture a future in which Elizabeth was subjected to Collins's conversation from dawn to dusk. And Darcy would only see her on his infrequent visits to Rosings, every year watching her bright spirit further dimmed by her husband's smothering presence.

At that moment, Collins reached out to brush a piece of hair from Elizabeth's forehead. Elizabeth flinched. Before Collins had lowered his hand, Darcy was striding toward them. He had not made a conscious decision to act, but his body had taken the choice from him.

Collins's voice faltered as Darcy approached. "Miss Elizabeth?" Darcy asked. "When we were talking of the improvements I planned for the garden at Pemberley, you had promised to show me the trellises on the south side of Longbourn. I understood from your mother they are particularly cleverly arranged." He gestured to the house.

In fact, their conversations had never ventured anywhere near the topic of gardens. Darcy only knew there were trellises because he had noticed them when approaching Longbourn from the road.

Elizabeth stared at him, bewildered. "The Pemberley gardens are very important to me," Darcy prompted.

Collins's gaze shifted between Darcy and Elizabeth as if he did not know what to make of the conversation.

Darcy offered his arm to Elizabeth. Collins, just as Darcy expected, dropped his arm, eager to please his patroness's nephew. The hard lines around Elizabeth's mouth immediately relaxed as she set her hand delicately at the crook of Darcy's elbow. It was not quite proper to offer his arm when she was already accompanied by another man, but Darcy cared nothing for propriety at that moment. His only goal was to rescue Elizabeth from boredom and mortification.

Darcy smiled down at Elizabeth. "Shall we?" he asked and steered her toward the south side of the house. Collins hesitated, took a step to follow them, and then stopped. *Good, let the man stand there and stew in his confusion.*

By the time they neared the trellises in question, Elizabeth had regained her composure. "Mr. Darcy, I am certain I would recall discussing our trellises with you." Her voice held a hint of amusement, and Darcy felt a secret joy at having restored her sense of humor.

"Please forgive the small deceit," Darcy said. "I thought you might wish for more exercise than the smaller garden would allow."

She shot him a sidelong glance. "Indeed. I thank you for your perspicacity."

"I am happy to be of service." Oh, how he wished he could be of service in so many other ways.

Darcy led her along the walk that passed by the trellises, and she obligingly told him which plants grew in which location. He could not get enough of the musical tone of her voice or the warmth of her hand on his sleeve. Just knowing that she was touching him, even through layers of wool, was a heady delight, but the brevity of this moment made it bittersweet.

Darcy's stomach roiled with nausea. What kind of future would Elizabeth have? He had not missed the mortified looks Collins's insipid and grandiose declarations had inspired. She was doomed to a life of shame about her husband. As a parson's wife, she might find meaning in caring for those in his parish, although Mr. Collins himself seemed to spend little time with his parishioners. And if they were blessed with children, she would make a splendid mother.

But she would endure years of stupid conversation and embarrassment at her husband's behavior. He would chastise her for her high spirits and demand that she keep her opinions to herself. Darcy shuddered at the thought.

And at night she would go to Mr. Collins's bed and surrender her body to him. Those images provoked a strong desire to strike Mr. Collins.

He pushed such thoughts from his mind, taking a deep breath and inhaling her scent. Instantly, his nausea receded. Now, however, he found himself imagining instead the prospect of Elizabeth in his bed. Oh, merciful heavens!

Darcy turned his gaze to the garden's collection of rose bushes, which were no more than a collection of dried twigs this time of year, and attempted to focus his mind on nothing other than rose cultivation.

However, speculation about Elizabeth's future life continued to intrude. Darcy had never visited the parsonage at Hunsford, but he had seen it. It was a modest abode, although in good repair, surrounded by gardens, and with a pig sty in the back. Elizabeth should not live in such a place. She should be…at Pemberley.

Perhaps Darcy should give up any attempts to turn his thoughts in another direction; they always returned to the same place.

Apparently having decided he wished to walk with his future wife after all, Collins came stumbling along the gravel pathway. Darcy suppressed a groan; he had hoped for meaningful conversation with Elizabeth during their walk.

She immediately dropped Darcy's arm but did not step close enough for Collins to claim hers. The sight of the rose bushes reminded Collins of Anne de Bourgh, and he proceeded to wax poetic about her many charms. Knowing his cousin as he did, Darcy was tempted to laugh. Anne might resemble a rose petal but only a brown, shriveled one—not a ripe, pink blossom.

Elizabeth listened to Collins's monologue, nodding occasionally but relieved of the burden to contribute to the conversation. *She will never be free of Lady Catherine's intrusion in her life, Darcy realized.   My aunt will tell Elizabeth how to dress, who to hire as servants, and what medicines to take when ill.* Some women might tolerate such constant instruction, but Elizabeth was too spirited.

She would never esteem his aunt for her rank alone. And his aunt's condescending attitude and lack of good understanding would never earn her respect from Elizabeth—the respect Lady Catherine felt to be her entitlement. It was a sign of Collins's idiocy that he had not realized how ill-suited Elizabeth was to the role of Lady Catherine's sycophant. Elizabeth's independent opinions and outspoken nature would horrify his aunt. They would despise each other.

Darcy stopped so suddenly he almost tripped.

He had hit on the solution!

To prevent Elizabeth from making a ghastly mistake, she must meet Lady Catherine *before* the wedding. Elizabeth might be determined to suffer Mr. Collins in silence, but surely Darcy's aunt would be too much of a burden. Once she met Lady Catherine, Elizabeth would understand how disastrous the marriage would be!

Yes, that was the key. They must meet. He had faith his aunt would not let him down. Now, he must find a way to get Elizabeth to Rosings…as soon as possible.

***

Mr. Darcy did improve upon acquaintance, Elizabeth reflected.

At times, she struggled to recall that Mr. Darcy was the man who had brought Mr. Wickham so low and that she should despise him for it. After having endured six days of his visits, she had seen little of the cold, haughty man she remembered from his previous visit. He had exerted himself to be kind and charming, appeared to enjoy her company and Jane's, and showed forbearance for her mother or younger sisters—although their company must have been wearing on him at times.

He did, however, remain barely civil to Mr. Collins, but she could not find it in her to condemn him too harshly for that.

Unfortunately for Mr. Collins, he suffered by comparison with Mr. Darcy. While not ill-favored, he certainly was not as handsome or tall as Mr. Darcy, but that would not have troubled Elizabeth had she truly loved the man. No, it was his conversation that most suffered by comparison.

Mr. Darcy was clever and well-informed, the very best sort of company. While he often said little, it was always to the point and of interest to Elizabeth. He took care to raise topics he knew would be of interest to her and Jane—and expected them to participate fully in intelligent discourse. Such an expectation should not have been surprising; however, enough men held such low opinions of a woman's intelligence that Elizabeth appreciated the distinction.

Mr. Collins, on the other hand, spoke a great deal more but said far less of import. By the end of three days, Elizabeth knew the entire history of the construction of Rosings, including the cost of nearly every individual element. She was far more familiar with the history of Rosings than she was with Longbourn's. Mr. Collins also took pains to acquaint her with the minute details of Lady Catherine's carriages, Miss Anne de Bourgh's illnesses, and the history of improvements to Hunsford Parsonage. She found herself drifting off twice—once during a description of the pig that lived behind the parsonage and the other during a long-winded discourse on the cleaning of the Rosings parlor carpet.

Mr. Collins's conversation was so plentiful, Elizabeth often found that she had simply ceased to attend to it and could not later recall what he had said. Perhaps her mind had begun to filter out the sound of his voice—which would be a danger to her if he were ever called upon to warn her that the house was on fire.

Mr. Darcy seemed to have an instinct for when Elizabeth was nearing her breaking point and would suggest a walk outside. Mr. Collins joined them infrequently since he was not a great walker and deemed the early spring weather too chilly, although Jane sometimes accompanied them. Elizabeth had attempted to foster some conversation between Jane and Mr. Darcy, thinking that perhaps he might have an interest in her—or develop one—if Mr. Bingley did not. However, he paid Jane no particular attention, and she treated him politely but not warmly.

Soon, these walks became the highlight of Elizabeth's day, as the only time she could escape both her fiancé and all thoughts of her encroaching nuptials. For the space of an hour or so, she could pretend that she was not betrothed to Mr. Collins and that she was simply Elizabeth Bennet of Longbourn.

However, she was well aware how soon these pleasant interludes must end; Mr. Darcy would not be available to accompany her on walks at Hunsford Parsonage.

Today, it was three days following Mr. Collins's arrival, and Elizabeth was feeling out of sorts for no good reason. Perhaps the cause was a brief quarrel with Mr. Darcy the day before. As they ambled through the garden, he had inquired if the militia was still in Meryton. When she had replied in the affirmative, he asked her to warn her younger sisters against Mr. Wickham.

Recalling what Mr. Wickham had said about how Mr. Darcy had treated him so infamously, Elizabeth bristled at the demand. She had allowed herself to be lulled by his apparent amiability, forgetting that he had abused his childhood friend so terribly. Smarting from her own lack of discretion, she had made a sharp remark about Mr. Wickham's misfortunes. Mr. Darcy had snorted and said, "Yes, his misfortunes are great."

"And of your making!" Elizabeth had retorted.

Mr. Darcy's face had turned white, and he had remained silent for some seconds; when he spoke, his voice was strained. "I do not know in what way Wickham has imposed on you, but I beg you to believe me when I tell you that his tales often contain only a small kernel of truth."

"Indeed?" Despite the tinge of desperation in Mr. Darcy's voice, Elizabeth had been prepared to challenge him, but Mr. Collins had arrived to claim her hand, and further conversation was impossible.

Elizabeth could not reflect on the conversation with satisfaction; indeed, it had weighed on her all night, rendering sleep difficult. She realized now that she had been quick to believe Mr. Wickham's story since it was in accord with her own observations about Mr. Darcy. But now that she knew the man better, she was more inclined to believe Mr. Wickham had perhaps made a mistake in understanding; she did not wish to believe him capable of outright deceit. The man he described did not seem to resemble the Mr. Darcy she was beginning to know. Once she had been content to place all the blame for Mr. Wickham's misfortunes on Mr. Darcy's shoulders, but now she began to doubt this assumption. Had she been too hasty? Although she was horrified to consider such an error in judgment, she owed it to Mr. Darcy to consider the possibility.

This dilemma occupied the whole of her thoughts as she kept her eyes fixed on her needlework, resisting the impulse to glance at Mr. Darcy across the room. Mr. Collins was recounting some advice Lady Catherine had given him about his sermons, and she could readily ignore the sound of his voice.

Then the door opened, and Hill announced that an express had arrived for Mr. Collins. This news struck the man momentarily—but all too briefly—speechless.

He hastily opened the letter and perused the contents. Then he looked at Elizabeth with a rapturous expression. "Cousin Elizabeth, a great honor has been bestowed upon you! Lady Catherine has invited you to visit her!" His voice held the reverence one might use for an audience with the Prince Regent or the Archbishop of Canterbury.

"Before we are wed?" Elizabeth asked, her heart sinking. She had little enough time left with her family before the wedding and did not wish to spend it traveling to and from Kent.

"Yes!" Mr. Collins raised the letter with a flourish and read aloud. "'I have heard so much about your future bride that I find myself very curious and desire to meet her. I am extending an invitation to Rosings for her to attend me Thursday next.'"

"Only three days from now!" Elizabeth's mother exclaimed.

Mr. Collins folded the letter and set it in his lap with a self-satisfied air. "This is a great compliment to you, my dear!"

"Oh, indeed, it is!" Mama declared, her hands waving about in excitement. "Who would have expected such condescension? Such regard? And before you are married! Oh, it is too exciting!"

"Naturally, I spoke of you when I was in Kent," Mr. Collins said. "And my letters to her have enumerated your many charms. But I never imagined she would bestow such an honor."

Elizabeth's throat constricted, and tears threatened to spill down her cheeks. She could see no graceful way to refuse the summons, for a summons it was. It would be a grave insult to turn down Lady Catherine's hospitality, and she could not afford to insult her future husband's patroness.

Mr. Collins and her mother regarded her expectantly. She swallowed. "Yes, it is a great honor," she agreed. Jane's eyes were full of sympathy. She understood Elizabeth's feelings about Mr. Collins and would guess she did not wish to visit Kent.

She noticed Mr. Darcy's eyes on her, but his expression was inscrutable. Did he find her lacking in enthusiasm? Then his eyes softened a bit, suggesting…if not sympathy, at least an understanding of her anguish.

Her mother's voice broke into Elizabeth's reverie. "I suppose you and Mr. Collins must travel by post. It is always so uncomfortable, but there is nothing for it."

Mr. Darcy straightened in his chair. "I would be pleased to take Miss Elizabeth and Mr. Collins into Kent. I have my carriage at Netherfield, and it has been some time since I have visited my aunt."

Elizabeth barely prevented herself from gaping at the man. Why would he make such an offer? He had not previously expressed a wish to visit his aunt. And he would be volunteering for hours of Mr. Collins's conversation. He had no need to do such a favor for Elizabeth. She could only conclude he was more attached to his aunt than she had previously suspected.

"That is very good of you to offer!" Mr. Collins exclaimed. "I am struck dumb by your generosity."

If only that were true! Fortunately, Mr. Collins did not appear to notice her inappropriate and hastily smothered giggle, but a corner of Mr. Darcy's mouth quirked up.

The master of Pemberley soon turned solemn again. "I see no reason for delay. We could leave as early as the day after tomorrow if that would suit."

"Indeed, that would suit admirably!" Mr. Collins's head bobbed up and down.

Mr. Darcy pointedly turned a quizzical look on Elizabeth when it became clear her betrothed would not solicit her opinion. "That would be fine," Elizabeth murmured, her voice cold to her own ears. She might as well get the wretched business over with. Perhaps it would only take a couple of days.

The reason for Mr. Darcy's sudden amiability remained a mystery to her, but perversely, it gave her another reason to dislike him. He might believe he was doing her a service, but deep in her heart, she felt that anyone who took her away from her family and helped her move into her life with Mr. Collins deserved no gratitude.

He nodded his head solemnly, but a small smile played about his lips. What was he so happy about?

Chapter 4

Mr. Collins snored.

Elizabeth attempted to ignore the snorting and snuffling emanating from the man as he slept, resting his head against the squabs of Mr. Darcy's elegant and well-sprung carriage. She could not travel alone with two unmarried men, so Mr. Bennet had decreed that Jane must accompany her. Jane had readily consented, and Elizabeth was pathetically grateful for the company.

Jane placidly embroidered, apparently unperturbed by the dying goose noises on the other side of the carriage. But Elizabeth found the snoring too irritating to concentrate on the book of poetry she had brought. Perhaps if she had not been staring into the future of her married life, such honking and rattling would not leave her so depressed.

Sitting across from her, Mr. Darcy simply glowered at the offending man, his eyebrows lowering with each snort. The carriage went over a particularly large bump. Mr. Darcy was jostled and somehow slid across the seat to Mr. Collins, jabbing the other man in the ribs with his elbow.

Mr. Collins gave a startled grunt but did not awake, settling back into a different position that, fortunately, allowed for a far quieter slumber. Mr. Darcy gave Elizabeth a conspiratorial smile as he maneuvered back into his place on the carriage seat.

"My ears thank you," Elizabeth said.

For a moment, he appeared to smile in response to her small joke, but she must have been mistaken. Mr. Darcy did not have a sense of humor, did he? However, he did lean forward in his seat, drawing her attention. "Miss Bennet, please forgive the impropriety, but I must give this to you."

A thrill of alarm shot through Elizabeth when she saw a letter in the man's outstretched hand. She reached out automatically to receive it. "Please read it, I beg of you." His eyes met hers briefly but then slid away again. "It touches on a topic we discussed two days ago."

Wickham. They had discussed many things, but only Mr. Wickham was important enough to be the subject of a letter.

Mr. Darcy glanced warily at Jane, but she had slumped against the window, her head bobbing with the rhythm of the carriage wheels as she slumbered. He cleared his throat. "I…I often do not say what I…in…I do not express myself well when I speak." His fingers worried the edge of his cuff nervously. "So I thought to commit my words to paper." His fingers drummed on his knee. "I hope you are not offended by the liberty."

"No, of course not."

His shoulders relaxed slightly, and he leaned back against the carriage's seat. *Does my opinion carry so much weight?*

"Would you have me read it now?" she asked.

He nodded, eyebrows raised. "Please."

Elizabeth broke the seal and read the letter. It contained a concise account of Mr. Darcy's dealings with Mr. Wickham. He detailed how they had been childhood playmates on the grounds of Pemberley and how his father had planned to grant his protégé the living at the estate. However, Mr. Wickham had asked for money in lieu of the living. Elizabeth was appalled to realize she had believed the man's lies and half-truths; however, she was horrified to read the next part. Mr. Wickham had attempted to seduce Mr. Darcy's sister and convince her to an elopement! When discovered, he admitted to only desiring her large dowry. *Oh, how awful for Miss Darcy!* She had narrowly avoided ruin; she must have been so angry and humiliated.

Elizabeth herself was embarrassed to think how she had been deceived by Wickham, but at the same time, she felt a peculiar and unexpected relief to know that Mr. Darcy was not the villain she had earlier believed. *Why does his true nature matter so much to me? It has little importance in my life.*

Finally, Elizabeth folded the letter and placed it in her lap. When she lifted her eyes, she was not surprised to find Mr. Darcy's gaze boring into hers. "T-this is an appalling account," she said.

He leaned forward, resting his arms on his thighs. "Do you believe me?"

She was startled to realize it had not occurred to her to doubt his veracity. "I—yes, of course. I cannot believe you would invent such a tale."

"Good." He straightened his spine, losing some more tension in his shoulders.

"Why did you say nothing before now?"

He grimaced, and for a moment, it appeared he would not respond. "I did not know the specifics of the rumors he spread about me. And I was hesitant to lay my affairs bare before others, but it is important that you understand the truth of the situation."

It is? "Why?" she asked.

He tilted his head to one side, regarding her with peculiar intensity. "Because you matter, Miss Bennet."

What an odd thing to say!

Elizabeth was about to ask him what he meant when Mr. Collins again shifted in his seat, and once more, his snores drowned out all conversation.

***

Darcy took a sip of tea, glancing about the drawing room with a sense of contentment. They had arrived at Rosings a few hours ago. So far, Lady Catherine had insulted Elizabeth's clothing, given her unnecessary advice on cold remedies, disparaged her musical abilities (without having witnessed them), and ordered Elizabeth to get blue curtains for the parsonage drawing room.

In other words, everything was perfect.

His aunt was living up (or down) to his expectations in every way. As the frequent object of Lady Catherine's biting tongue and condescending attitude, Darcy was pleasantly surprised how easily he could turn these qualities to his advantage.

The letter he had written to his aunt about Elizabeth was a masterpiece of indirection. He had not disparaged Elizabeth but had spoken of her lively spirit and independent opinions frequently enough to provoke Lady Catherine's disquiet. An invitation to Rosings was the result.

Lady Catherine presided over the drawing room in a throne-like chair, with his cousin, Anne, and her companion seated to her right. Darcy sat next to Anne. On the other side were arrayed Collins, Elizabeth, and Miss Jane Bennet.

Mr. Collins sat on the very edge of his chair, almost literally hanging on every word from Lady Catherine's mouth. He treated each utterance as if it were a gemstone of incalculable value to be admired and cherished.

Miss Jane Bennet's expression was less serene than usual. Her lips were pursed so forcefully they were turning white, and she turned an anxious glance on Elizabeth almost once a minute. His aunt was quite talented to have managed to disturb those placid waters.

And well she might. Lady Catherine might not recognize the signs, but Elizabeth had a hold on her composure by a thin thread. The muscles of her jaw and neck strained as she held her chin unnaturally high; her body was stiff and straight in the ornate, brocaded chair she sat upon. At least twice, she had been on the verge of speaking before pressing her lips firmly closed. A third time, she seemed primed to explode, but a warning look from Collins caused her to subside.

Darcy could have grabbed Collins and shaken him for that alone. Who was he to tell Darcy's Elizabeth what she could say in company?

Lady Catherine was delivering a soliloquy about the proper way for a young lady to come out into society. Her imperious gaze landed on Elizabeth. "Are any of your younger sisters out?"

"Yes, ma'am. All," Elizabeth replied. Her words were terse, bitten off.

"All!" cried his aunt. "What, all five out at once? Very odd! The younger ones out before the elder are married? Your youngest sister must be very young." Lady Catherine employed her most disapproving tone of voice and waved her hand like a queen sending someone to be beheaded.

"Indeed!" Collins's head bobbed up and down like a child's toy.

"Yes, the youngest is not yet sixteen," Elizabeth replied. "Perhaps she is full young to be much in company." Lady Catherine looked mollified by this admission; however, Elizabeth continued speaking. "But, really, ma'am, I think it would be very hard upon younger sisters that they should not have their share of society because the elder may not have the means or inclination to marry early."

Collins looked as if he had witnessed a terrible carriage accident. His hand covered his mouth as if he wished to take back Elizabeth's words himself. Lady Catherine's expression was one of sheer amazement. How long had it been since someone so decidedly below his aunt's station had contradicted her opinion? This might be an entirely new experience for her.

For a moment, Darcy feared his aunt might need her smelling salts, but she recovered enough to grimace at

Elizabeth. "Upon my word, you give your opinion very decidedly for so young a person. Pray, what is your age?"

Elizabeth smiled in a disarming way. "With three younger sisters grown up, Your Ladyship can hardly expect me to own it."

Darcy had taken an ill-advised sip of tea and barely managed to swallow without laughing. There was no reason for Elizabeth to conceal her age; she was hardly on the shelf, but she had clearly lost patience with Lady Catherine's overbearing attitude and was doing her best to thwart his aunt at every turn.

Yes, it would not be long before Elizabeth begged off the engagement. He felt a moment of regret for subjecting her to this ordeal, but she should learn of these difficulties now—when she could act on any reservations—rather than after the wedding.

Lady Catherine's voice had lowered to a growl. "You cannot be more than twenty, I am sure. Therefore, you need not conceal your age."

Elizabeth regarded the lady for a minute as if weighing the advisability of another pert retort, but finally, she said simply, "I am not one and twenty."

Lady Catherine gave a small, dignified nod, acknowledging this information—or perhaps she was granting Elizabeth permission to be twenty years of age.

With a sniff, she dismissed Elizabeth from her concerns and turned her attention on Collins, launching into detailed instructions about his next sermon. However, her narrowed eyes frequently darted to Elizabeth. Lady Catherine did not appreciate being crossed by a "country nobody."

Elizabeth's capacity for defying his aunt only added to her charms where Darcy was concerned. However, Collins's face suggested that he was having the opposite reaction. No doubt he would lecture Elizabeth later on "proper deportment." The thought made Darcy's body tighten, and his hands clenched into fists.

Soon, Lady Catherine signaled her intention to withdraw for the night, and everybody rose to depart. Mr. Collins would return to the parsonage, but Miss Bennet, Elizabeth, and Darcy had all been given guest rooms at Rosings.

Before she turned to go, his aunt turned her gaze on Elizabeth. "I will take you to the shop tomorrow so you may purchase that blue fabric I mentioned. It would not do if they have sold it all."

Recognizing the danger, Collins laid his hand on Elizabeth's forearm, in what he no doubt believed was a soothing gesture. Darcy started forward with the goal of forcibly removing Collins's hand from her person but caught himself after only one step. Collins had the right to touch her, and Darcy had none. Meanwhile, Elizabeth swallowed, and her hands clenched the skirt of her dress as she attempted to gain mastery over herself. But the effort was futile.

Elizabeth's eyes flashed as she met Lady Catherine's gaze. "I would prefer yellow curtains in the drawing room." Her voice was level but firm.

His aunt literally flinched at this unexpected news, her mouth hanging open in a most unattractive way. "Yellow? Do not be absurd. Blue is a far better color for a south facing room."

"I thank you for your opinion." Elizabeth smiled, but there was no warmth in it. "I appreciate your solicitude for our well-being, but it will be my house, and I prefer yellow." Darcy suppressed an urge to applaud.

Before Lady Catherine could respond, Elizabeth slipped away from her and stole into the front hallway. "Good night, Your Ladyship." Jane followed her sister, and their light tread could be heard as they ascended the grand staircase.

His Elizabeth was made of stern stuff indeed. Darcy admired her forbearance but was impatient for her to realize the impossibility of her situation. Until she cried off the engagement, he could not act in good faith.

Lady Catherine's shocked gaze followed the two women out the room. When they had disappeared, she exploded. "I am not accustomed to such impertinence in my home!"

Darcy could not help defending his beloved. "The parsonage is to be her home. I do not believe a preference for yellow curtains can be construed as impertinent."

Collins spoke over him. "I will speak with her, Your Ladyship. She is young. I will have her understand the deference due your rank."

Lady Catherine ignored Darcy and nodded imperiously to Collins. "You do that."

Darcy bristled on Elizabeth's behalf, but remained silent. Ultimately, the worse Lady Catherine treated Elizabeth, the more it served Darcy's purposes. When he had concocted the scheme, however, he had not realized how difficult it would be to watch his beloved endure his aunt's tirades.

Soon, he vowed, he would make her Mrs. Darcy, and she would never have to endure such misery again.

***

Elizabeth tore at her bonnet ribbons and slammed the unoffending garment on the chair next to the doorway. "Insufferable woman!"

Sitting by the window in the sitting room they shared, Jane kept her focus on her embroidery. "I take it you are speaking of Lady Catherine?" Her mild tone was no doubt intended to calm Elizabeth's nerves.

"Yes! *Mrs. Jenkinson* says nothing, so she had done nothing to offend me!" Elizabeth paced the length of the room and back. "Lady Catherine, however, believes I should wear my hair differently and criticizes Papa for not engaging a governess. Today, she even found fault with the bows on my dress!"

"Oh, dear." Jane finally set the needlework in her lap, regarding Elizabeth with a furrowed brow.

"Indeed!" Elizabeth stalked to and fro; her encounter with Lady Catherine had produced a great deal of excess energy. A walk outside would help calm her agitation, but she might encounter Mr. Collins, Mr. Darcy, or the lady herself. Who knows what she might say in her present state of mind? "Mr. Collins simply nods as rapidly as possible and agrees with whatever she says. I am beginning to suspect his head is not properly affixed to his neck."

"Lizzy!" Jane covered a laugh with her hand.

"Then there is Mr. Darcy!" Elizabeth exclaimed. "He is neither a fool nor a tyrant. I believe he is embarrassed at his aunt's bad manners and annoyed with Mr. Collins's insipidity. Yet he does nothing to blunt his aunt's rudeness. He simply observes with that slight smile on his face!" Elizabeth's skirt tangled as she walked, and she yanked the fabric so roughly it nearly tore. "He is enjoying himself. Just like Papa!"

Jane had an abstracted air about her as she considered this. "No, he is not like Papa. Mr. Darcy watches *you* a great deal."

Elizabeth rubbed the back of her neck, trying to ease the tension. "True. I am certain he seeks to discover my defects, although I know not why he bothers. His aunt is quick enough to enumerate them."

"Perhaps he admires you," Jane suggested.

"Mr. Darcy?" Elizabeth burst into laughter. "The man who cannot look on a woman without finding fault?"

Jane shrugged, not joining in Elizabeth's merriment.

The anger had drained from her, leaving only weariness. Elizabeth collapsed into the chair next to Jane's. The weight of her situation pressed down upon her. "Oh, Jane, what can I do? When I marry Mr. Collins, Lady Catherine will be my neighbor, and I must see her several times a week!" In general, Elizabeth had avoided thinking about the inevitable event, but this recent encounter in the Rosings's drawing room had stoked her anxieties.

Jane's eyes remained fixed on her needlework. "Have you considered if perhaps you should not marry Mr. Collins?"

Elizabeth caught her breath. Jane did not know the precarious state of their father's health and surely did not understand her decision. Elizabeth let out her breath slowly. "I must. I cannot choose otherwise."

"Longbourn is not worth your happiness," Jane said.

No, but the future of my family is.

"I will grow accustomed to Lady Catherine and my circumstances," Elizabeth said, regretting that she had voiced her unhappiness. "It is simply different from the life I knew. If I am determined to bear it, I can. I am not formed for ill-humor." She tried to imbue her words with a confidence she did not feel.

"Oh, Lizzy!" Jane's anxious expression brought tears to Elizabeth's eyes.

Elizabeth reached out and patted her sister's hand. "All will be well. Mr. Collins has promised I may visit Hertfordshire frequently."

"But Lady Catherine—"

Elizabeth smoothed her skirts, not meeting Jane's eyes. "My difficulty is that I provoke her. Mama always tells me to hold my tongue. I did not fare so well today, but I will do better in the future. I will."

I must.

***

Although Rosings Park was certainly a grand house, Elizabeth found little to admire about it. The architecture was uninspired, and the décor was overly embellished, making most of the rooms feel heavy and dark. At times, she longed for the simplicity of a plain wooden chair or a sturdy unadorned staircase. However, Rosings did boast two redeeming features: the beautiful grounds and the library.

Only five days into their visit, Elizabeth had already wandered the grounds until she was footsore, so she had taken herself to the library. Although the décor was less baroque than the rest of the house, the room was still remarkably ugly—covered in dark paneling that needed dusting and lit by grotesquely shaped wall sconces. It did boast an astounding number of books, but the collection was uninspired and old. There were no modern authors or poets, and the older books appeared to have been untouched for decades.

The chief virtue of the library was its emptiness. Despite describing herself as a devoted reader, Lady Catherine apparently eschewed books. Anne de Bourgh might have the time to read but not the inclination. *What did the young lady do with her time?* Elizabeth wondered. Perhaps she took a prodigious number of naps. But the library's loss was Elizabeth's gain, and she enjoyed the solitude the room afforded her.

Of course, the library did have a full set of William Shakespeare's works, and Elizabeth had delighted herself with old favorites. On this particular day, she had curled up in a chair near the window and was smiling at some of the witty banter in *Twelfth Night*. The staff had laid a roaring fire despite the mild weather outside, and Elizabeth found it overly warm.

The library door opened. "Ah, there you are Cousin Elizabeth!" Elizabeth had grown better at concealing the winces when her fiancé addressed her.

She marked her place and set the book down, mustering a smile. "Mr. Collins."

At least he had not started the conversation by calling her "best beloved" or "dearest one." His insistence on using extravagant terms of endearment often made her head ache. Bizarrely, it drew her attention to how little they knew each other.

His false smile was plastered on his face as usual, but as he closed the distance between them, she noticed unaccustomed agitation in his features and energy in his movements. "I must speak with you!"

Elizabeth's mind turned to horrible events. Jane injured. A sister eloped. Her father—no, she must not allow her imagination to run wild!

Her breath caught. "Is there something wrong?"

"No, no." Mr. Collins shook his head vigorously. *At least it is not a family illness.* Elizabeth sagged back into her chair.

Then he tipped his head to the side and considered. "Well, yes, but no, not precisely. I suppose one might term it a problem, but I am convinced it will all work out for the best." His patently false smile only deepened her irritation. Why could the man not simply say his piece and leave her to her books?

"May I be of some assistance?" she asked.

"No. Well, yes. Yes. Well, no, I suppose 'help' is not precisely the proper word." He paced back and forth in front of her chair.

Elizabeth barely refrained from rolling her eyes. "Pray tell me the problem, sir."

Mr. Collins ceased pacing, regarded at her with an expression akin to panic, and cleared his throat. "Well, er, yes. I was speaking with my esteemed patroness, Lady

Catherine de Bourgh." He said the name grandly as if Elizabeth were in danger of forgetting it. "And she condescended to give me some advice."

Oh, this cannot be good.

"She expressed some reservations about whether your naturally lively spirits and outspoken nature were entirely suited to be the wife of a man of the cloth." He spoke with an air of foregone conclusion; now that Lady Catherine had expressed an opinion, then it must be so.

Elizabeth's stomach lurched sideways. She had not anticipated this conversation, this event.

"And I thought that perhaps you and I were too hasty—caught up in our youthful ardor—"

Despite her dawning sense of uneasiness, Elizabeth bit her lip to keep from laughing at this wildly inaccurate portrayal of their relationship.

"I find myself in agreement with Her Ladyship. I need a wife better suited to the sedate living of a country parson—and perhaps one more grateful for the condescension of Lady Catherine de Bourgh."

He is breaking off his engagement with me! The horrified realization swept through her mind.

Mr. Collins's eyes avoided Elizabeth's and remained fixed on his hands, which tugged fretfully on his cuffs. He had made a decision about Elizabeth's future based on the opinion of someone wholly unconnected to her—and without considering, or even discussing, Elizabeth's options or opinions. No wonder he could not meet her gaze.

Elizabeth was aware that she should try to persuade him against this course of action, but shame paralyzed her tongue. Her heart was beating a rapid rhythm, and her face grew hot, although she could not say if she was more angry or mortified. Jilted by Mr. Collins! What would everyone think of her? What would she say upon her return to Meryton?

Suddenly, she realized that Mr. Collins still addressed her. "This is quite disappointing, my dear. I know it was your fondest wish—and mine as well, of course—to be united, body and soul! And you can be by no means certain another proposal of marriage will ever be made to you. It grieves me deeply, but Lady Catherine does not believe it would be prudent to continue on as we were."

Elizabeth clenched her teeth against a dozen angry retorts that crowded her mind. Collins was breaking off their engagement because she was not sufficiently sycophantic to that overbearing, shrewish woman! How could he?

He continued speaking, but Elizabeth paid no heed. Shame was giving way to despair. Her family's future was once more in jeopardy! If her father died suddenly… Elizabeth swallowed back her tears and covered her mouth with her hand.

"Oh, my dear cousin, I have wounded your delicate sensibilities. I know this has come as a shock!" Mr. Collins bent over, hovering so close to her face that she was forced to lean back in the chair. "I know how eagerly you had anticipated our conjugal felicity!"

Suddenly torn between laughter and a need to retch, Elizabeth turned her face from him and focused on the window overlooking the garden. Mr. Collins was mercifully silent for a minute, and Elizabeth concentrated her attention on slowing her breathing.

Mr. Collins dithered back and forth, apparently unnerved by the sight of a distressed woman. "Perhaps you are in need of a vinaigrette?" he asked.

Elizabeth shook her head. She felt many things, but an inclination to swoon was not one of them. Primarily, she felt a need to escape Mr. Collins's presence. "Maybe I will take a turn in the garden." She kept her eyes downcast so he could not read her expression. "Some fresh air will do me some good."

"Yes! Fresh air!" Mr. Collins seized on this excuse to dispose of her inconvenient emotions. "Just the thing to mend a broken heart!"

"Indeed," Elizabeth murmured. "'Tis a wonder Wordsworth has not already composed a poem on the subject." At least she was now relieved of any burden to be agreeable to the odious man.

Elizabeth stood quickly before he could decide she *was* in need of smelling salts. However, before she could take a step, Mr. Collins was next to her, lending completely unnecessary support under her elbow. Fortunately, the library boasted French doors that led directly to the garden. Mr. Collins shadowed her every step as she walked to the door.

A blast of cool spring air greeted her, and she savored the smell of forsythia and cherry blossoms. She paused on the threshold, unsure how much longer she would be able to maintain a façade of civility to Mr. Collins. "I would prefer to be alone in the garden."

"Yes, of course. Of course!" Mr. Collins finally released his death grip on her elbow. "Solitude can assuage your tears. And fresh air. And flowers. Perhaps you will see some butterflies this time of year…"

Elizabeth was torn between a desire to laugh at the man and run from him. Not only did he believe she had formed deep feelings for him in a short time, but he also thought those feelings could be overcome by a walk in the garden. "I pray you, leave me alone."

She swiftly marched away, relieved to hear the snick of the latch behind her.

Confident she was no longer observed, Elizabeth sank onto an intricately carved stone bench near the center of the garden, under a weeping willow. Her entire body seethed with warring emotions. Despite the flood of anger and shame, she was also giddy with relief to be released from this unpleasant duty. But the relief itself provoked guilt. She had accepted the proposal for good reasons, and those reasons persisted.

Now she had lost the betrothal that was to be her family's salvation. Lost the opportunity to keep Longbourn in the family. Lost the means of supporting her mother and sisters when her father passed on. And there could be no mistake; it was her fault. She must be impertinent. She must speak her mind to Lady Catherine.

Once word reached Meryton, she would be the object of gossip for months. Everyone recognized Mr. Collins for a fool. If he had jilted her, who would want her? Her reputation would be seriously damaged, if not destroyed.

Elizabeth balled her handkerchief up in one hand.

How would she tell Papa?

How would she tell Jane?

Then the tears arrived.

Chapter 5

Darcy had enjoyed a long ride about the grounds of Rosings, a blissful two hours fantasizing about taking Elizabeth to Pemberley—without his aunt's voice to intrude or importune him. The day had grown warmer, and he longed for a tall glass of lemonade or perhaps some tea.

Even a recent letter from Bingley had done nothing to diminish his good spirits. His friend had warned Darcy that Miss Bingley had determined to visit Pemberley on her hastily arranged "tour of Derbyshire" —a thinly veiled scheme to prevail upon Darcy even though he had not extended an invitation.

Bingley had decided to accompany his sister in the hopes that he could control her behavior; they were likely *en route* to Pemberley already. Darcy had written to warn Georgiana of the impending intrusion and given her permission to decamp to London if she desired. Miss Bingley would be surprised to arrive at Pemberley to find no Darcys in residence, but she deserved nothing less.

Entering the house through the gardens and the library improved Darcy's odds of avoiding his aunt and her hints about his "engagement" to Anne. The soles of his boots crunched on the gravel of the garden path as he strode toward the house. Darcy brushed sweat-dampened hair from his brow, thinking longingly of the day he would be free to leave Rosings and return to Pemberley.

By this point in the visit, he had hoped Elizabeth would already have broken off with Collins, yet she had gritted her teeth through several encounters with his aunt and shown no signs of wavering in her determination to wed the man. *Her determination is something you admire about her,* he reminded himself. Certainly, Jane Bennet would never stand up to his aunt in such a fashion, but he wished Elizabeth would be somewhat less stubborn on this point.

Darcy had almost reached the French doors leading to the library when he heard a strange noise.

A sob. Someone was crying nearby, in the garden.

Whoever it was, she was trying to be quiet, but the muffled sounds carried across the soft spring air. Probably it was simply a housemaid who had been reprimanded for breaking a saucer; Lady Catherine could be quite severe on her staff. Another sob and a sniffle. *Not your concern.* Darcy reached for the door handle.

Would someone on Lady Catherine's staff feel free to avail herself of Rosings's garden? No, his aunt would not look kindly on such liberties. Therefore, it followed that the sobs came from someone in the family or one of her guests. Another matter entirely.

Darcy dropped his hand and turned back toward the garden. Not wishing to alarm the quiet crier, he slowly paced down the pathway until he approached a break in the hedges where he could view a large expanse of the garden in one glance.

Blast and damnation! It was Elizabeth. From his hidden spot, he could see her huddled on a bench a few yards away. A tear-stained face, red swollen nose, and bloodshot eyes were visible only for a moment before she again buried her face in her handkerchief.

What had happened? An illness or death in her family? But no, then she would be preparing to depart for Hertfordshire. A quarrel with her sister? That seemed highly unlikely.

Perhaps his aunt had said something unforgivably cruel. That was more plausible. Or Collins. His judgments about Elizabeth's family could be most heartless. Darcy fought against an impulse to strangle whoever had caused that look of despair on the face of his beloved Elizabeth. She should never suffer so.

As he watched, Elizabeth tried to gather herself. She lifted her head, dabbed her eyes with her handkerchief, and swallowed hard, willing away the tears. For a moment, she appeared to succeed through sheer will, but then twin tears trickled down her cheeks, and a great sobbing breath wracked her body. Dropping the now-sodden handkerchief in her lap, she again buried her face in her hands.

It was too much for Darcy. He made no effort to muffle the sounds of his boots as he hastened along the pathway to the bench. Elizabeth did not lift her head as he neared. Had she remained oblivious to his approach, or was she hoping the intruder would leave her in peace?

He sat next to her on the bench and wordlessly offered her a handkerchief. Elizabeth lifted her eyes briefly and quickly glanced down again, no doubt trying to hide her reddened eyes. "Oh, Mr. Darcy!"

He pressed the handkerchief into her hands; after a moment's hesitation, she used it to dab at her eyes. "Miss Bennet, you are unwell. Is there anything I can do for your present relief?" he asked.

"No, I am quite well, thank you." This obvious falsehood, uttered as it was into the handkerchief, nearly provoked Darcy to laughter.

"Perhaps your sister—"

"No!" Elizabeth cried, looking at him wildly. Then she blushed, settling back on the bench. "Forgive me. I did not mean to sound so—"

"Have you quarreled?"

"With Jane?" Elizabeth laughed. "I believe she is constitutionally incapable of quarrelling with anyone."

"I am certain my aunt would find a way," Darcy said darkly.

Miraculously, this utterance elicited a chuckle from Elizabeth. "No, I must tell Jane my sad news eventually, but I cannot face her just yet...."

Now Darcy was even more mystified about the cause of her tears. It was almost as if Elizabeth was ashamed of something, but what could it be? And how could he learn the truth? Any question he could ask seemed intrusive.

"Perhaps I could bring you some wine?" he asked. "Or help you into the house for some rest?"

"I thank you, no." Elizabeth shuddered. "I could not bear to enter Rosings at this moment."

Darcy nodded. "The décor *is* rather overdone. However, it is unlikely to change in the immediate future."

Elizabeth exhaled a laugh. "Why do you persist in making me laugh when I have every intention of remaining miserable?"

Darcy congratulated himself on lightening her mood. If only she would divulge the reason for her distress! "Is there nothing I can do to help?"

Elizabeth stared down at her lap. "I thank you for your solicitude, but no. It would be best if you leave me in peace. This too will pass, as my aunt always says." The moment of levity had passed, and her eyes were once more shadowed.

"But—"

"I beg of you, please leave me in peace!" Elizabeth's voice was strangled with emotion.

The thought that Elizabeth did not wish his comfort tore his heart in two. *Now I am truly paying for my earlier arrogance!* Darcy longed to put his arms about her and have her rest her head on his shoulder, but propriety would not allow it—and more to the point, she would not wish it.

Aside from her sister, there was no one at Rosings who might comfort her. The thought of Mr. Collins being any use was laughable. What a terrible husband he would be!

"I beg you!" Elizabeth hissed again.

Darcy's limbs were heavy with reluctance as he stood and took a few steps away from the bench, but he stopped. He could not do it. He could not leave his beloved in such a state. Even if she never spoke of her anguish, at least she would know she was not alone. *I will stay until she is no longer seized by distress.*

Darcy withdrew a few yards from Elizabeth, pacing on the gravel and regarding her face. A few minutes passed. Although she was no longer sobbing, tears trickled down her cheeks. Darcy felt in his pockets and produced another clean handkerchief, which she accepted with downcast eyes.

"You need not remain." She struggled to keep her voice level, but he discerned a slight shakiness. "This business is not of your making. And I will not perish here next to the hydrangea bushes from a few tears!"

Darcy smiled at her slight jest. "I cannot, in good conscience, leave you in this state. I understand the matter is private and will not intrude. But do not desire my absence. You should not be alone at such a time."

Elizabeth shook her head, wiping a tear with the tips of her fingers. "I cannot make out your character at all. Every time I believe I have, you thwart my understanding. You are quite the conundrum." She managed a watery smile.

At least she could manage a ghost of her previous teasing tone! "As I live to vex my acquaintances, I am pleased to hear of my success."

This provoked an actual chuckle from Elizabeth. "How do you make me laugh at such a time?" However, her expression quickly slid once more into despair. The impulse was so strong to take her into his arms and soothe her troubled spirits, but Darcy settled for sitting next to her on the bench. At least she no longer seemed to object to his presence. "Is there nothing I can do?"

Elizabeth sighed; the hands in her lap twisted his handkerchief into different shapes. "Very well, I cannot conceal the unhappy truth for long.... Mr. Collins has broken off our engagement."

"What?" Darcy did not realize he had shouted until Elizabeth flinched. "Does the man have no honor? How could he—?" If the parson appeared before him at that moment, Darcy would have been quite pleased to strike him.

Elizabeth kept her eyes cast at the ground. "Lady Catherine persuaded him that I do not have the proper temperament to be a parson's wife." Elizabeth's lips twisted into a wry grin. "I daresay she is right."

"And he did not give you an opportunity to break it off instead?" Darcy demanded. Elizabeth looked up at him, blinking. Clearly, this thought had not occurred to her. Having been jilted by a fiancé would seriously damage Elizabeth's future marriage prospects and would make her the target of gossip for years, whereas Collins's reputation could easily have survived the indignity of Elizabeth rejecting him. Darcy choked back some choice epithets.

He pushed his hand through his hair. *Damnation! This is* my *doing. I maneuvered my aunt into inviting Elizabeth. I encouraged my aunt's disapproval and enjoyed Elizabeth's impertinence.* Yes, he had hoped to end the engagement but felt not the slightest impulse to congratulate himself on his success. He had expected to open Elizabeth's eyes to the foolishness of the match and provoke her into action. He never suspected Collins would be so cowardly or care so little for his cousin's reputation.

How was it possible that Darcy had made things *worse* for Elizabeth when all he wanted to do was lay the world at her feet?

He leaned forward, resting his hands on his knees, taking the opportunity to view Elizabeth more closely. She was no longer crying but was staring at nothing, her face pale and wan. If he had a hope of alleviating her distress, he must know the precise cause.

He chose his words with care. "Forgive me for asking, Miss Bennet, but I had not supposed your attachment to Mr. Collins was so deep."

She gave a little laugh and turned her face to him. Even with red eyes and a swollen nose, her beauty could not be diminished. "Is that a polite way of inquiring why I would attach myself to a foolish, insufferable man?"

Darcy suppressed a smile. Only Elizabeth would be so frank. "I would not put it in such words...."

"You may not know that Longbourn is entailed upon Mr. Collins. Marrying him would have ensured that my family could continue to reside there after my father's death."

"That is a great sacrifice to ask of you." He strove to maintain a neutral tone. How could her father have put her in such a position?

Darcy expected her to demur and claim it was nothing. She hesitated, staring at a rosebush across the path. "No one *asked* it of me. I love my family very much."

Even as he seethed with anger at her situation, his heart was full of admiration for her self-sacrifice. *Not that I need another reason to love her.* "Surely there are other ways to secure your family's future?" *Such as marrying me?*

She gave a rueful laugh. "I suppose I may have as many charms as most women, but I do not possess much of a dowry, and that is the charm that entices most men."

His insides knotted even more tightly. "And why should the burden fall to you? What about your sisters?"

His tone earned him a sharp look from Elizabeth, and he attempted to arrange his features into a more disinterested expression. "My younger sisters are too young and do not take their responsibility seriously. And Jane..." Elizabeth's eyes darted quickly to Darcy and then down to her lap. "Jane's heart was engaged elsewhere. I would not ask this of her." Another tear rolled down her cheek.

Darcy understood her furtive glance. She believed her sister had harbored a *tendre* for Bingley; perhaps she still did. Had he been wrong in encouraging Bingley to leave Hertfordshire? Darcy had thought Jane Bennet's heart was not touched, but this was not the first time that Elizabeth had hinted otherwise. And he had not failed to notice how the older sister seemed out of spirits or how she flinched when Bingley's name was mentioned.

If she did love Bingley, then Darcy had done his friend—and her—a grave disservice. He winced at a sudden realization. If he had not interfered with Bingley and Miss Bennet, they might now be betrothed, and Elizabeth might not have felt the necessity of accepting Mr. Collins's offer. Truly, he was being punished for his interference!

Elizabeth watched him, one eyebrow raised. "Mr. Darcy?" His face must have displayed a hint of these self-recriminations.

He rubbed the bridge of his nose. "It is nothing of import." He would ruminate on Bingley and Miss Bennet later. For now, he must focus on Elizabeth's dilemma. "Surely your family will understand that Mr. Collins's whims are not your fault. They will not blame you." Even as he uttered the words, Darcy recognized they were cold comfort.

"My father will not. My mother…" Elizabeth shrugged. Remembering Mrs. Bennet, Darcy knew she could easily twist this situation to be her daughter's fault.

"You and your sisters are still young. Surely there is no need for such haste in selecting husbands," Darcy observed. After Georgiana made her debut, he had no intention of pushing her to marry right away.

This seemingly innocuous observation provoked more tears from Elizabeth. "There is more need for haste than one might assume." Her tone was brittle, and Darcy feared he had made a misstep.

Oh, Good Lord! Was she suggesting that her father was seriously ill? Darcy massaged his forehead with one hand. He had heard nothing of an illness but now realized he had not seen Mr. Bennet during his many visits to Longbourn.

If her father were to die in the next months, Elizabeth and her sisters would indeed be in dire straits. Without the security of Longbourn and its income, they were even less likely to make good matches, and their fortunes could fall quite quickly. Where would they even live? Small wonder Elizabeth was so distraught over the loss of even an idiotic fiancé.

His chest tightened further, and his heart thumped wildly. *What have I done?* He prayed fervently that she never learned of his role in her trip to Rosings Park.

Of course, he could easily solve Elizabeth's financial concerns with a marriage proposal, but these were hardly the circumstances for such a delicate conversation. Her face was tear-streaked, and her hair was in disarray. Although the garden was lovely, conversation about Mr. Collins and her family's finances had contributed to a rather dismal atmosphere.

More to the point, Darcy was not at all sure she would accept him. Although her opinion of him might have improved over the previous week, she might still view him as stiff and arrogant, and any association with his aunt did him no favors.

But if she was willing to accept Collins, surely she would accept me. Yes, her family's situation meant that the chances she would refuse him were small. Surely marriage to him could not possibly be more unbearable than to the garrulous parson.

However, Darcy's skin crawled at the very thought of being compared with that odious toad. They were in no way alike, except for their admiration for a pair of fine eyes.

More importantly, Darcy hoped to secure her acceptance because she loved him, not because her family needed security. He wished to have her love—or at least her affection—before offering marriage, but at this moment, the best he could hope for was tolerance.

While he had been woolgathering, Elizabeth's sobs had started anew. *I am altogether useless! I cannot even help her stanch her tears.*

He took another handkerchief out and handed it to her. She accepted it with a self-deprecating roll of the eyes. "I am sorry to be such a watering pot! I am not usually so—"

"No need to apologize," he interrupted. "What Mr. Collins did was dishonorable and cruel. Naturally, it was a shock."

Elizabeth stared down at the handkerchief. "It will be horrible when word reaches Hertfordshire. Mama told everyone how I was to marry Mr. Collins. Now I will be a disgrace. The greatest fool in England does not want me for his wife. What could possibly be so wrong with me that even a man like him would not want me? My whole family will be a laughingstock!"

Darcy swore a hundred silent curses.

"My sisters will find it more difficult to make good matches. I sought to improve my family's situation, and I have worsened it!" Another tear trickled down her cheek.

Now Darcy cursed his aunt. He should have foreseen her interference; it was entirely consistent with her character. But he had been so caught up in his resolute desire to secure Elizabeth's consent that he had not considered all the possibilities. And now Elizabeth would suffer for it. Naturally, being jilted would cause disgrace to her family. He shuddered to think of what would be said in Meryton.

He paused his ruminations to realize Elizabeth was staring at some rose bushes without seeing them. "Miss Bennet?"

"No one yet knows Mr. Collins has broken off the engagement...." Her voice sounded thin and far away. "Perhaps I could convince him to change his mind—persuade him that I will be a quiet, biddable wife." A knife twisted in Darcy's gut. *She would try again?*

Elizabeth stood slowly, wiping away a final tear. "But he would not make such a decision in opposition to Lady Catherine." Her gaze turned to Darcy. "Perhaps if you spoke with her, you might persuade her to change her mind. You could assure her I would do everything in my power to be the kind of wife her parson needs."

Darcy stifled a groan. He could think of fewer requests more distasteful to him, but Elizabeth's imploring, grief-stricken eyes were difficult to meet without some measure of remorse. He wished to help her, but...no. Everything in him rebelled against advocating in favor of such a marriage. He could not dissemble to that extent.

He rubbed the back of his neck, damp with sweat. How could he possibly respond without revealing everything? "I apologize, but I cannot do so in good conscience." Her brows crinkled together in perplexity. "I do not believe he is the right husband for you." *That would be me.*

For a moment, Elizabeth simply regarded him, her lips slightly parted. Would she argue the point? Would she march off to convince Collins of his grave error? What if she succeeded despite Lady Catherine's opposition?

If she planned to approach Collins once more, Darcy must find a way to stop her. He would propose if necessary—even under less than ideal circumstances with an unsure outcome. He would take that chance rather than risk losing her forever.

Elizabeth's lips twisted into a bitter smile. "Is that your true opinion, or do you share your aunt's estimation of my character?"

Darcy barely choked back an oath. "Nothing could be further from the truth!" Elizabeth recoiled slighted at the vehemence of his tone. "There is *nothing* wrong with you, save that you are far too good for Mr. Collins!" He struggled to get his anger under regulation. "He is too selfish a creature to make anyone a good husband."

Elizabeth regarded him with a small frown. Was she so surprised to receive a compliment from him? Had he created such a terrible impression? Then her shoulders slumped, and she cast her eyes downward. "Few will share your opinion. This news will cause my parents great distress."

"You need not tell them immediately," he heard himself murmur.

Elizabeth's head jerked up. "I cannot lie upon my return to Longbourn! Surely you do not expect me to remain in Kent, sir? There is nothing to keep me here now. I will write to my aunt and uncle in London and hope we may travel to their home tomorrow."

Darcy ran his hands through his hair and cursed himself for a fool yet again. He had voiced the suggestion without considering all the consequences. She could hardly return and allow everyone to believe she continued her engagement with Mr. Collins. He was not surprised she wished to quit Rosings Park immediately, but the thought of being separated from her caused a hollow ache in his chest. The pain doubled at the thought of Elizabeth exposed to gossip and speculation.

Damnation! He had hoped that by the time she broke off the engagement, she would be prepared to accept an offer from him. The slight scandal of jilting Collins would be lost in the excitement of her marriage to the master of Pemberley. He considered again whether he could propose now, but her morose face suggested his first impulse had been right.

Still, he could not send her to Meryton. Perhaps she could stay in London with her aunt and uncle? However, there was no reason for her to linger there; she might return to Hertfordshire at any time.

If she did not return to Longbourn, where could she go?

Aha!

How to phrase this? Darcy cleared his throat. "I feel Mr. Collins has made a grave misjudgment and that my aunt has done you a terrible disservice. Unfortunately, both my aunt and her parson are rather set in their ways; I do not believe their minds could be changed on this matter. However, I might lessen the blow, at least temporarily. I was planning to go from here to Pemberley, my estate in Derbyshire. Would you and your sister do me the honor of being my guests?"

Elizabeth stared at him for a moment. "Pemberley?" she repeated blankly. Had the offer tipped his hand? Did she recognize his interest in her? Panic welled up at the thought she might reject him before he had a chance to redeem his behavior.

"Yes, I had been hoping to introduce you—you and your sister, that is—to my sister, Georgiana." Aware that he was babbling, he finally managed to close his mouth.

"Your sister?" Elizabeth's expression was thoroughly bewildered. The opportunity was slipping away from him. "I thank you, but—"

Darcy interrupted before she could refuse. "And there will be other guests you number among your acquaintances. Mr. Bingley and his sisters will be visiting us." Darcy fervently thanked the heavens for Miss Bingley's grasping nature, which he had been cursing only an hour before.

"Mr. Bingley!" Elizabeth's eyes lit up for the first time. Darcy felt a flash of jealousy despite knowing her delight was on her sister's behalf. If only she showed such enthusiasm for *his* company! "It would be lovely to see him again—and his sisters, of course."

Darcy managed to suppress a satisfied smile. The fish had taken the bait.

Elizabeth bit her lip, her eyebrows furrowed in concentration as she considered his invitation. "But Papa expects us home directly…"

"You need only visit for a few days." Darcy kept his voice low and soothing.

"No, it is too much to ask of you."

"You are not asking; I am offering. My aunt is partially responsible for your current predicament. I cannot have her compensate you for the wrong she has done, but I can make amends on behalf of my family."

Elizabeth bit her lower lip in a way that Darcy found utterly endearing. "I should like to see Pemberley, and it would be lovely to see Mr. Bingley again."

She wished to see Pemberley? Darcy's whole body was filled with an unexpected warmth, and he felt an almost maddening impulse to call for a carriage and carry her off to Derbyshire that minute.

Elizabeth and Pemberley…the combination was…intoxicating.

"I am certain your father would like you to have an opportunity to travel and form acquaintances," he said.

Her eyes were on him, but her thoughts were clearly occupied by the possibilities presented by a trip to Pemberley.

"We can have a maid accompany us if you would be more comfortable," he added.

She gave a quick shake of her head. "It will not be necessary, thank you." She swallowed. "I will speak with Jane about your invitation. If she sees no impediment, I will be happy to accept. Of course, I must also write to my parents...."

"You will come to Pemberley?" he asked, practically vibrating with excitement.

"Yes." She gave him a gracious smile.

He stood. "Good! I will write to my housekeeper tonight when to expect us."

Elizabeth struggled to her feet as well. "I thank you, it is a most gracious offer. You are being far kinder to me than I deserve."

Darcy took a step toward her and then stopped. "No, indeed, Eliz—Miss Bennet. You deserve far more." He noted her puzzled look before he turned and strode toward the house.

***

The next morning, Elizabeth was busily packing her trunk when the maid informed her that Mr. Collins awaited her in the sitting room. Unable to comprehend what could possibly prompt a visit to her private quarters, particularly before seven, Elizabeth also solicited Jane's company since they shared adjoining rooms.

The Bennet sisters had barely seated themselves before Mr. Collins launched into the purpose of his visit. "Dear cousins, Lady Catherine has condescended to offer her coach this morning to take you as far as Brompton. And from there, you can engage a post to London where I understand your uncle resides."

Elizabeth exchanged a glance with Jane. They had not discussed any travel plans with Mr. Collins the night before. Both ladies had claimed fatigue and taken trays in their room rather than join the others for dinner. Apparently, Mr. Darcy had not shared his plans with his aunt either.

"I thank you for your solicitude, Mr. Collins," Elizabeth began. "However, I—"

Mr. Collins waved his hands in agitation. "I know you are loath to depart from Rosings Park—"

Elizabeth nearly laughed; she had never been so eager to quit a place in her life.

"However, Lady Catherine asked me about your plans this morning. I believe she is eager to have the house to herself. Miss de Bourgh finds guests so tiring."

Elizabeth took a deep breath rather than voice her opinion of Lady Catherine's hospitality. It was abominably rude to essentially disinvite guests in such a way! Anne de Bourgh had not troubled herself to say a word to either of the Bennet sisters, so Elizabeth hardly thought their presence bothered her.

"I appreciate your concern," Elizabeth said again. "But it is unnecessary."

Mr. Collins frowned, making him look like a wizened old man. "I assure you, Her Ladyship will not look kindly on it if you overstay your welcome."

Elizabeth bit her lip before an angry retort emerged. "We have no intention of doing so. Mr. Darcy has generously offered to transport us in his carriage this morning."

The parson's head jerked in surprise. "Mr. Darcy? But—He—" Mr. Collins swallowed. "I-I did not realize he was departing. He will take you to Brompton?" Yes, her cousin found it troubling that Mr. Darcy saw the Bennet sisters as worthy of his attention in any way.

Despite herself, Elizabeth felt a corner of her mouth curl into a smile. "No, he has invited us to visit him at Pemberley."

For a moment, she feared her cousin was about to fall off of his chair, but he managed to grab the arm in time. "Pemberley? But he-he cannot possibly—" Mr. Collins spent several moments casting about for reasons why they could not undertake a journey he knew would meet with Lady Catherine's disapproval. "I cannot imagine by what means you imposed yourself on Mr. Darcy, but it is not proper!" he finally concluded triumphantly.

Elizabeth opened her mouth for an angry retort but then noticed movement behind Mr. Collins. Mr. Darcy had entered the room through the door Mr. Collins had left open. *Oh, dear! How many of the insulting accusations had Mr. Darcy heard?*

"I assure you, Mr. Collins, the trip to Pemberley was entirely my doing." Mr. Darcy crossed the room to stand beside Elizabeth. "If anything, it was I who imposed upon Miss Bennet." He took her hand gently in his. "I had quite despaired when she accepted your offer, but now that she is free again, I have another opportunity to press my suit." Mr. Darcy tenderly laid a kiss on the back of her hand while his eyes never left her face.

On Elizabeth's other side, Jane gasped—a sound Elizabeth barely discerned over the pounding of her heart. It took her a moment to collect her wits while she gaped at him. But then she realized he must be joking—teasing Mr. Collins. Nevertheless, the look on his face took her breath away. It was hard not to be affected by the naked desire in his eyes even though she knew it was in jest. *Yes, of course, it was all an act.*

Mr. Darcy placed another lingering kiss on her hand but then turned his head to regard the other man. "I must thank you, for you have given me hope." Elizabeth stifled an urge to giggle. She had never suspected Mr. Darcy to possess such well-developed thespian skills.

With his mouth agape and his eyes wide, Mr. Collins resembled a fish—or perhaps a cow chewing its cud. "Y-you—sh-she—and—what?"

"Before yesterday, I believed she thought me the last man in the world she might be tempted to marry," Mr. Darcy explained patiently. "I am much obliged to you for discontinuing the engagement. Now I may cede that title to you!" He concluded with a grand smile that suggested Mr. Collins had indeed received an honor.

"Y-yes, yes. I see," Mr. Collins responded as if Mr. Darcy's gratitude were real.

"It is early yet to make an offer so soon after you jilted her, but I am hoping to persuade her to a courtship." Mr. Darcy's conspiratorial smile seemed to take the other man into his confidence.

"Indeed?" Mr. Collins took out his handkerchief and mopped his brow.

Elizabeth watched this exchange with amazement. Mr. Darcy's behavior was scarcely believable coming from a man who usually seemed as serious as a monk. His eyes, lit with humor, met hers briefly, and his lips quirked upward. If Mr. Collins had not treated her in such an infamous manner, she might have been tempted to take pity on him.

He was now trembling all over. "Does Lady Catherine know?" he asked Mr. Darcy in a horrified whisper.

Mr. Darcy shook his head. "I thought it best not to mention it." Then he tapped a finger thoughtfully to his lips. "And now that I think on it, perhaps it would be best if you were not present when she learns of it. She may feel it would have been preferable for you to continue your betrothal." Elizabeth was almost sorry that she would not witness Her Ladyship's reaction. If she actually believed the farcical tale of Mr. Darcy wishing for Elizabeth's hand, Lady Catherine would bitterly regret interfering in Mr. Collins's marital felicity!

The man in question had turned quite white and appeared to be in danger of swooning. "Y-yes! Yes, indeed!" Mr. Collins staggered to his feet, searching frantically around the room. "Where is my hat? Oh, I believe I left it downstairs! I must go at once! Oh, dear me! Perhaps a visit to my sister is in order—" He was still babbling as he struggled out the door; his voice grew softer and softer as he hurried down the hallway.

Elizabeth could no longer contain her mirth. "This trip has been full of disappointments but also unexpected amusements!" she observed to Mr. Darcy.

Jane was the sole of discretion and patience, but even she had a smile, although it was concealed behind her hand. "Oh, dear, I hope he does not suffer an attack of apoplexy from the excessive worry!"

Mr. Darcy threw himself into a chair. "Any suffering will likely be of short duration and is no less than he deserves! The man has no honor." He scowled at the doorway through which the parson had departed.

"Really it was very bad of him to break his promise to Lizzy in that way," Jane observed. "Although one cannot but feel sorry for the abuse he will suffer at Lady Catherine's hands."

"I beg your pardon. One can help feeling sorry for him." Elizabeth lifted her chin. "He shall reap what he has sown." She sighed, leaning back in her chair.

"But, Lizzy, why did you not mention—?" Jane glanced between her sister and Mr. Darcy.

Elizabeth feigned amusement she did not feel. "Mr. Darcy was merely teasing Mr. Collins. We have no understanding." She glanced at Mr. Darcy, awaiting his corroboration.

He seemed lost in thought, staring at the fireplace, and only noticed their attention after a moment. "Er…yes, of course." Abruptly, he straightened in his chair and focused his gaze on Elizabeth. "I merely wished to remind him of your true worth—what he has given up. You are a great prize that any man should be pleased to win."

Anyone, but not Mr. Darcy, Elizabeth observed. Uneasy under the force of Mr. Darcy's gaze, Elizabeth looked down at her lap, realized her hands were picking at the lace on her dress, and forced them to lie still. "You are too kind," she murmured.

The man frowned anxiously, his gaze sweeping over Jane and landing on Elizabeth. "I apologize if my…joke with Mr. Collins made you uncomfortable."

Elizabeth cleared her throat. "No, indeed, it was quite a merry joke. And I must confess I do not mind if Mr. Collins suffers a bit of disquiet."

Mr. Darcy shifted in his chair. "My thought precisely."

Yes, of course. Mr. Darcy was angry with her erstwhile fiancé for his lack of honor in jilting her. It was a sense of chivalry that prompted his jest—and a desire to make Mr. Collins uneasy. Nothing more.

Of course.

But it was all so strange.

***

When Mr. Darcy wanted something to happen, it could happen very quickly. Trunks were packed, and carriages were made ready for travel. By ten in the morning, they were ready to leave. Elizabeth was quite impressed by the efficiency of his servants.

Although Lady Catherine seemed disturbed to be losing her nephew's company, she was also relieved to be rid of Elizabeth's troublesome presence in her house. Mr. Darcy had not mentioned continuing on to Pemberley, and it was probably best that Lady Catherine remained in ignorance about that part of the plan. Not surprisingly, Mr. Collins had made himself scarce.

Elizabeth had considered writing to Longbourn to explain the end of her betrothal to Mr. Collins. However, her heart quailed at the thought of delivering such tidings to her parents. Her father would worry about the family's future security without Mr. Collins. What might the shock do to her father's heart?

They would likely only visit Derbyshire for a few days, and during that time, it was not probable that her family would hear any news of the broken engagement from another source. In the meantime, Jane could see Mr. Bingley. Perhaps by the time they returned to Longbourn, happy news would balance the sad news of her disgrace.

Mr. Darcy was eager to reach Pemberley, so their route took their carriage around London and into the northern country fairly swiftly. They had eaten a lunch packed by Rosings Park's excellent cook. Early afternoon sun flooded the carriage, making it rather warm inside. Jane had devoted her attention to her embroidery but finally succumbed to the sway of the carriage and fell asleep with her head on Elizabeth's shoulder.

Elizabeth still experienced some doubts about the wisdom of accepting Mr. Darcy's invitation, although Jane had endorsed the plan. Why had he troubled himself to invite them? She could only guess that he wished to bring Jane and Mr. Bingley together again.

Mr. Darcy had been quite solicitous of her feelings in the garden and concerned about her comfort since then. She had expected the broken engagement would only confirm his low opinion of her and had been shocked when his reaction had been horror at Mr. Collins's callous treatment and chagrin at his aunt's role in it. Clearly, she had not appreciated before the degree to which honor and a sense of justice provoked Mr. Darcy's actions.

Undoubtedly, the cold, unpleasant Darcy would reappear at some point—most likely when they reached Pemberley. She and Jane had provided entertaining company when the society at Rosings Park offered few alternatives; certainly, she believed their conversation was more interesting than Lady Catherine's or Mr. Collins's. But when Mr. Darcy was among other, more appealing guests, he might regret his overly generous impulses toward her, and she would be subjected to his disdain again.

The thought made her feel sad for some reason, and she immediately chastised herself for it. One moment of amiability could not lull her into a false sense of friendship with the man. She could not depend on his friendship. If she did, she would only be disappointed. She had not expected much from Mr. Collins, and yet he had still managed to disappoint her. No, she could only rely on Jane and other members of her family. If Jane benefited from the trip to Pemberley, it would be worth everything.

Elizabeth enjoyed the passing scenery from the carriage window, but Mr. Darcy, seated opposite her, was making her uncomfortable. Often when she happened to glance his way, she noticed his gaze on her.

After a while, Elizabeth could not bear the silence between them and engaged Mr. Darcy in some innocuous conversation about the weather and the state of the roads; then their dialogue faltered. Still, Mr. Darcy persisted in giving her heated looks from under the brim of his hat. Elizabeth felt herself grow warm and uncomfortable. What did he mean by watching her so? She refused to be intimidated! The thought made her smile.

"You find something amusing?" Mr. Darcy asked.

She supposed a version of the truth would do. "I was reflecting that you have a way of making things happen," Elizabeth replied, careful to keep her tone distant and neutral.

He arched a brow quizzically. She explained, "You wished to leave Rosings Park, so we did. You wished to take us to Pemberley, so we are on our way. You wished to lessen the burden of Mr. Collins's rejection, and you have, most admirably."

A crease formed between his eyebrows. "Is this a bad quality?" he inquired. Naturally, he was too intelligent not to notice the potential criticism in her observation.

"Not in the main, no," Elizabeth responded. "I would imagine it is a desirable quality for many. However, some people in your position might be tempted to bend others to their will."

Both his eyebrows rose. "Is *this* flaw to be laid at my feet as well?" Was it possible he was hurt by her implication? No, he could not possibly care so much for her opinion.

"I do not know you well enough to say."

Mr. Darcy covered his mouth and coughed. "You overwhelm me with your flattery." When he removed his hand, a smile curved the corners of his mouth.

"Do you require my flattery?" she asked archly. "Others might fulfill that role more ably than I." She kept her tone from being overly friendly; it was far too easy to be drawn into an easy banter with him.

"I do not require it, but I would like to believe I have earned your admiration at least in some ways." His smile had disappeared. Was he in earnest? Did he really desire her good opinion? Why? No, most likely this was simply empty chatter, a little meaningless flirtation to pass the time.

She could play that game as well. "*My* admiration? Of what use is it to you?" she asked with a cool smile.

He paused for a long moment, and she thought he might not answer. "I do not believe it is very liberally bestowed and, therefore, all the more worth the earning."

Elizabeth tilted her head to the side and regarded Mr. Darcy quizzically. Did he truly believe his words or was he only seeking to flatter her? *No, I cannot afford to believe he cares for my opinion.*

"Or, am I mistaken?" Mr. Darcy's voice recalled her to the conversation.

"No, I suppose there are few people I think well of and even fewer I could be said to admire," she conceded, casting her gaze down at her hands. But then she reflected on the statement; how arrogant it made her sound!

"It is wise not to form judgments too quickly." Mr. Darcy's voice had a rough edge she could not identify. "But I will not importune you with questions about where I stand in your opinion. Hopefully, this trip will help improve me in your estimation."

Elizabeth's head shot up, but for once, Mr. Darcy's gaze was directed out the window at the passing scenery. His expression was shuttered and unreadable, although the rapid drumming of his fingers on his leg betrayed some tension. Had he sensed her dislike for him, or had someone mentioned it to him?

"From what I have heard of Pemberley, an invitation to visit would be enough to raise its master in anyone's estimation," Elizabeth replied, striving to lighten the tone of the conversation.

Mr. Darcy's gaze slid back to Elizabeth. "I am sure that is not true of everyone." *Did he mean her?* "And I would rather win admiration through the content of my character."

"Surely we all wish that," she replied.

"I cannot imagine any would find fault with your character." He regarded her steadily as he spoke.

Before Elizabeth had a chance to reply to this rather enigmatic statement, she felt Jane stir next to her and raise her head. "Oh, Lizzy, I believe I fell asleep! I shall have such a horrid crick in my neck now!"

Elizabeth had never before been so pleased to have a conversation interrupted.

Chapter 6

Darcy was ready for a career on the stage. After three days on the road with Elizabeth and her sister, he had become a master at concealing the thrill he experienced simply from being in her presence. His heart raced, and his pulse quickened just at the sight of her face. However, Elizabeth's reactions to *him* gave him cause for unease.

She spoke to him with her usual sportive manner, and he would not have it any other way. But she gave him none of the flirtatious smiles or shy glances so common to women who hoped to attract a man's attention. Was her pert conversation itself a kind of flirtation? Or was she truly uninterested in his particular attention?

When she had agreed to visit Pemberley, Darcy had hardly been able to contain his excitement. In fact, he had focused his efforts on not kissing her right there in Rosings's garden. He was aware that only Bingley's presence had induced her to accompany him, but he hoped that her acceptance had indicated a softening of her attitude toward him, a demonstration that she was developing tender feelings for him. Yet nothing in her actions or conversation since then had sustained that hope.

Furthermore, he seemed to be doing a pathetic job of altering her opinion of him; indeed, he was singularly ill-suited to recommend himself to the woman he loved. He completely lacked that felicity of manners Bingley or his cousin Fitzwilliam—or even Wickham—displayed so easily. They could laugh and charm a lady, and he could only sit in a carriage while brooding and glaring at her. Why *would* Elizabeth wish to tie herself to him?

Darcy could only pray that the environs of Pemberley would soften her attitude. He knew she loved to walk; fortunately, Pemberley boasted some of the finest grounds in England, and he intended to make the most of them, even if he must walk her over every square mile. He could not keep the Bennet sisters in Derbyshire long without giving rise to rumors, but Darcy did not wish to let Elizabeth go without securing her consent to an engagement. However, he was increasingly at a loss about how it could be achieved.

To complicate matters, as they neared Pemberley, Darcy was finding it increasingly difficult to contain his emotions. So often he had fantasized about bringing Elizabeth to Pemberley, showing her the grounds, making her the mistress of the house, leading her to his bed... The closer they drew to his ancestral home, the more such fantasies haunted his thoughts, making it difficult to think of anything else. He found himself staring at her neck, her well-formed fingers, her delicate ankles...

No! He must banish such thoughts. He could not allow his feelings to overcome him.

Rationally, he knew there was no cause for Elizabeth to dislike Pemberley. She had disapproved of Rosings Park's ostentation, but Pemberley did not share that fault. However, in his frequent moments of self-doubt, he agonized that she would find a reason to dislike the place—as she once disliked him. If she detested Pemberley, all was lost; he could not offer her a life apart from his treasured home. Or perhaps she would feel Derbyshire was simply too far from Longbourn? Had that been part of Mr. Collins's appeal? Kent was an easy distance from her family. What if mere geography stood in their way?

Darcy's hands were clenched in tight fists, resting on his thighs; he made a conscious effort to relax them. A surreptitious glance at Elizabeth showed her gazing out the window without having noticed his nervous mannerisms.

Only then did Darcy realize the carriage had already entered the grounds of Pemberley. Caught up in his own thoughts, he had failed to notice. *Had they already passed the spot?* He took a quick look out the window. *No, thank goodness!*

Both women had their eyes fixed on the scenery, eyes darting among the different sights. Elizabeth was not smiling but did not appear to disapprove of the view. At least it seemed to hold her interest. Darcy turned his gaze from her; it would not do to be caught staring. But only moments later, he realized his eyes had drifted back, still preoccupied with her face.

They were at the place. Darcy banged on the roof for the carriage to halt.

The ladies turned to him quizzically. "This is the first place on the road from which you might view the house, and it is framed to advantage from this spot," he explained, gesturing for them to peer out of the right window.

Darcy was immediately rewarded by the admiration in Elizabeth's eyes. "I do not believe I have ever seen a house so happily situated." Darcy was caught between a swell of pride and an immense sense of relief.

"Thank you, Miss Elizabeth."

"Indeed," Miss Bennet breathed. "It is magnificent!" Darcy murmured thanks to her as well.

"It is quite the handsome building." Elizabeth's eyes had not left the house. Darcy basked in her praise, all the more precious for being so rarely bestowed. Now if only her eyes would shine so when she gazed on him! "However, I do not believe I can accurately evaluate its worth without knowing the cost of its chimney piece."

He thrilled at the sly glance she cast his way. She was teasing him! Darcy laughed. "I have not made a study of such things, but I may be able to produce the information after some searching."

She bestowed on him one of her bewitchingly arch smiles. "I would not put you to any trouble." Her gaze was drawn back to the window. "The grounds are beautiful. Do you have formal gardens?"

"Yes, they were my mother's pride and joy." Darcy peered at the lowering sun. "We may not have time to see them today, but I would be pleased to give you a tour tomorrow."

A small crease was forming between Elizabeth's brows when she turned back to him. "That would be lovely, thank you." Her tone was somewhat bemused, but he did not know why. Surely she understood how pleased he was to have her at Pemberley!

"If you have seen enough here, there is another excellent view a little further on." Darcy rapped his walking stick on the roof, and the carriage continued on its journey.

***

Although she knew Mr. Darcy's temperament was far different to his aunt's, Elizabeth had still expected Pemberley to resemble Rosings Park in its décor. However, as the carriage approached the front entrance, the house was revealed to be grand but without pretention. Its lines and proportions were elegant, and it was set perfectly within the surrounding grounds. No doubt the interior would be similarly free of the gilt details and excessively baroque ornamentation so prevalent at Rosings. Despite being difficult and unpleasant, Mr. Darcy was a man of refinement and taste.

Several footmen hastened out of the entrance as the carriage approached, followed by a simply dressed girl whom Elizabeth guessed was Mr. Darcy's sister. A broad grin demonstrating her eagerness to see her brother, she rushed down the path with far less decorum than Elizabeth would expect from the kind of haughty girl Mr. Wickham had described.

As soon as the coach rolled to a stop, Mr. Darcy threw open the door and jumped out so he could embrace his sister. Elizabeth exchanged glances with Jane. Who would have believed him capable of such exuberance? The more time she spent with Mr. Darcy, the less she felt she actually knew him.

A footman placed a stool next to the carriage, and Mr. Darcy immediately released his sister so he could help the ladies out, introducing each in turn. Georgiana Darcy's expression grew far more reserved as she greeted the strangers, but Elizabeth could see this was the result of shyness rather than pride.

As the sisters greeted Miss Darcy, a tall figure came bounding out of the house like an eager puppy. Mr. Bingley! He pumped Mr. Darcy's hand vigorously and bowed to the all the ladies. However, his gaze was immediately drawn to Jane, who blushed and looked down when their eyes met. But her lips formed a soft smile. Was she embarrassed at Mr. Bingley's attentions or concerned that their reunion would be the subject of gossip and speculation?

Mr. Darcy was completely still, observing his friend and Jane—his expression inscrutable. Did he disapprove? Would he try to separate them? No, surely not after he had gone to some trouble to bring them together again!

Others emerged from the house at a more sedate pace. Elizabeth stifled an urge to groan. Miss Bingley was gliding toward the party in a gaudy orange gown far more ornate than required by the occasion.

"Mr. Darcy!" Miss Bingley drawled. "It has been too long since we have seen you!" She lifted her hand to him as if expecting him to kiss the back of it. His face carefully blank, Mr. Darcy had little choice but to follow suit. However, he seemed displeased at being forced into the position. Mr. and Mrs. Hurst followed and exchanged greetings with the group—Mr. Hurst with a bored, half-awake expression and Mrs. Hurst with a sneer. Miss Bingley's greeting to Jane was superficially warm, but Elizabeth was not fooled.

Mr. Bingley beamed happily at everyone, but Mr. Darcy's expression suggested he was pained by his guests' ill manners.

Then Miss Bingley greeted Elizabeth. "My dear Eliza! It is so good to see you again!" Elizabeth pressed her lips together rather than respond sharply to this unasked for familiarity. It would have been so much more pleasant to visit Pemberley without Miss Bingley's presence. But she was happy Mr. Bingley was here, and she was willing to suffer his sister for Jane's sake.

Miss Bingley made a show of looking around. "Was your betrothed unable to accompany you? I am sorely disappointed! I will miss his delightful conversation." Behind her sister, Mrs. Hurst covered her laughter with her fan.

Elizabeth winced. She had forgotten that Mr. Bingley's sisters knew about the engagement. "Mr. Collins remained in Kent." She would need to explain the circumstances eventually but hardly felt equal to the task at the moment.

"What a shame!" Miss Bingley exclaimed. "I am sure you will love Pemberley as I do, although unfortunately, one cannot plumb its depths in a single, short visit! I am certain, however, there are plenty of muddy walks." Miss Bingley looked sidelong at her sister with a sly smile.

Elizabeth had to admire Miss Bingley's economy with words. In only two sentences, she had managed to remind Elizabeth that she had never visited Pemberley before—while Miss Bingley had—and that her visit was likely to be solitary and brief. Not to mention recalling the incident with the petticoat and the mud.

Mr. Darcy approached, clearing his throat. Elizabeth felt her face heat. Had he heard Miss Bingley's mortifying comments? Would he join in their merriment at her expense? Of course, she did not care about his good opinion, yet somehow the thought of his ridicule made her heart shrink.

Mr. Darcy's face was pale, and his gaze was fixed on Miss Bingley. "Unfortunately, many of my guests do not care for walking. However, Miss Elizabeth has such a fine appreciation for the outdoors, I am very much looking forward to showing her Pemberley's grounds." His expression remained carefully blank, but the rebuke in his tone was unmistakable. "And I hope it will be the first of many visits."

"Y-yes." Miss Bingley regarded him somewhat uncertainly. "How delightful."

He immediately turned to give instructions to the footmen. What could he mean? Why would he think Elizabeth would ever return to Pemberley? She had been stunned to be invited just once!

Miss Darcy led the way to the house, and the guests followed. Mr. Bingley offered Jane his arm as they walked. Of course! Mr. Darcy anticipated that they would marry, and Elizabeth would be invited to Pemberley as the new Mrs. Bingley's sister. *I could grow to enjoy visits to Pemberley, but I do not believe I will ever like being related to Miss Bingley!*

***

Darcy cursed silently. He had hoped for some private conversation with Elizabeth once they were no longer traveling, but he had not anticipated how disruptive Caroline Bingley would be. Each of her cutting remarks made him grind his teeth.

By the time they arrived at Pemberley's great front hall, Miss Bingley had somehow contrived to insinuate her hand onto his arm. It had happened while they were walking, and he had been too startled to prevent it.

Damnation! It would give Elizabeth the wrong impression.

The front hall was quite magnificent, boasting two sets of Italian marble stairs and an ornate ceiling decorated with fan vaulting. He had hoped the sight would take Elizabeth's breath away. Darcy and Miss Bingley were the last of the party to enter the hall, so he craned his neck to get a glimpse of Elizabeth's expression. She stood off to the side and in shadow, actively examining the room's décor but not smiling. Did she feel it was overly ornate? Or was she still smarting from Miss Bingley's barbs?

Following the direction of his gaze, Miss Bingley's eyes narrowed as she noticed Elizabeth. She tugged on his arm a little to remind him that he should pay attention to her. "Oh," she announced loudly, "it is lovely to be back at Pemberley! It is quite like a second home to me."

"I am so pleased to hear you say that," Darcy said. "You will have no trouble finding your way about, so I may devote my efforts to the first-time visitors." He dropped Miss Bingley's arm and strode off to join Elizabeth.

***

After the new arrivals had refreshed themselves, the party gathered in the music room for tea and entertainment before dinner. Unable to contain himself any longer, Darcy had finally asked Elizabeth to play the pianoforte, and basked in the emotions she produced from the instrument. Perhaps she did not possess the greatest technical proficiency, but no one could fault the expressiveness of her playing. He would never tire of listening to her.

While Georgiana and others in the party shared Darcy's delight, the same could not be said of Miss Bingley. She sat very straight in her chair, with her lips firmly pursed, refusing to even glance toward the pianoforte. Instead, she stared straight ahead as if hoping Elizabeth would evaporate if ignored for long enough. If it was socially acceptable to put her fingers in her ears, no doubt she would have done so.

Elizabeth finished her piece, and everyone applauded as she arose from the bench. "Will you favor us with another song?" Darcy asked.

She smiled sweetly. "I should take a rest and allow others to play, though it is a fine instrument." Immediately, she took a seat in one of the brocaded chairs near the fireplace.

Miss Bingley stood abruptly, drew herself to her full height, and strode to the piano bench. Perhaps she was seeking to intimidate her perceived rival, but Elizabeth looked more amused than cowed. The other woman seated herself at the piano bench with a great flourish, carefully adjusting its position to suit her needs.

"Miss Bingley, would you like me to turn pages for you?" Elizabeth asked.

"That will not be necessary." Miss Bingley did not trouble herself to look at Elizabeth. "I know the piece from memory."

Elizabeth lost none of her composure at this set down but nodded and exchanged an amused look with her sister. Miss Bingley commenced to play a complicated piece of baroque music, which demonstrated her mastery of the instrument but remained cold and unemotional.

Everyone applauded at the end of the song, except for Mr. Hurst, who had fallen asleep again. Darcy feared Miss Bingley would begin another song, but she stood and graciously gestured to Georgiana. "My dear Georgiana, surely it is time for you to entertain us!"

Darcy was alarmed to see his sister shrinking into the upholstery of her settee. "No, I pray you. Do not ask me." Her voice was practically a whisper.

Usually, Georgiana could steel herself to the necessity of performing before strangers. Did Georgiana believe her playing could only suffer by comparison to Miss Bingley's? Darcy wished he could reassure his sister that her abilities far exceeded the other woman's.

"There is no need to be shy! You are among friends!" Miss Bingley stalked toward Georgiana, holding out a hand. Always in possession of an ulterior motive, she must have believed that Georgiana's playing would further intimidate Elizabeth. How dare she use his sister to further her jealous goals?

Elizabeth shot to her feet. "Miss Darcy, perhaps you would prefer to wait until after we have practiced the duet we discussed this afternoon?"

Georgiana frowned. Elizabeth kept her eyes locked on Darcy's sister, nodding her head slightly. "Yes, I would prefer that," Georgiana said finally. Darcy would have wagered money that his sister and Elizabeth had never discussed a duet.

Elizabeth turned her gaze on Miss Bingley. "So Miss Darcy will entertain us another day. Did you have another air you would like to play? If not, I know one or two pieces that I believe would be suitable."

Miss Bingley's face could have been carved from stone. She had been outmaneuvered by Elizabeth and could do nothing but accept defeat. Elizabeth's graciousness in the face of her victory was probably interpreted by Miss Bingley as rubbing salt in the wound.

"I would favor the group with another piece," she ground out, glaring daggers at her rival.

"Lovely!" Elizabeth resumed her seat, the picture of alert interest. Georgiana watched Elizabeth with shining eyes. *She does have that effect on Darcys.*

It had occurred to him that Elizabeth's lively disposition might help Georgiana overcome the despair she experienced since the Ramsgate affair. And it appeared that the relationship was well on its way to being established. Now if only he could get Elizabeth to accept the attentions of another Darcy…

***

Soon, Carter, Pemberley's butler, announced that dinner was to be served, and the assembled party adjourned to the dining room. Before they were seated, Georgiana pleaded a headache and retired to her chambers. She dismissed her brother's expressions of concern and insisted they continue with the meal as planned.

After the party had been seated at the table, Miss Bingley continued her sly attacks on Elizabeth. "Will you have a pianoforte when you move to the parsonage?" she inquired, her voice full of false solicitude.

Darcy ground his teeth. The woman was once again drawing attention to the difference in their stations. Elizabeth had said nothing of her broken engagement with Mr. Collins; perhaps she felt needless shame over having been jilted.

Elizabeth regarded the other woman with tolerable composure. "The parsonage does not have an instrument, but when I visited Rosings Park, Lady Catherine offered me the use of her pianoforte there."

Darcy admired how Elizabeth neatly avoided mentioning the broken engagement and implied an intimacy with Lady Catherine that had never existed.

Miss Bingley switched tactics. "And how will you enjoy being a parson's wife?" She made no attempt to keep the sneer out of her voice.

Elizabeth's eyebrow lifted as she regarded Miss Bingley steadily. "I believe the clergy to be full of some of the best men in England, who have answered God's call to administer to those in need. Therefore, being a clergyman's wife is also a noble calling—helping to care for the poor, sick, and desperate. It is an admirable use of a woman's time and talents."

Darcy noticed that a smile had spread itself over his face. Miss Bingley made no immediate response but flipped open her fan and commenced to fan herself with unnecessary rapidity. Trust Elizabeth to disarm Miss Bingley through a sincere admiration for those clergy who had a true calling to the profession, although Darcy doubted that Elizabeth would number Collins among that group.

For the next few minutes, silence reigned over the table as everyone applied themselves to their repast. However, Miss Bingley's pinched expression suggested she had not missed the implicit rebuke in Elizabeth's response, and indeed, a second attack was not long in coming. "Your parents must have been pleased you made such an advantageous match." She smiled condescendingly at Elizabeth. "And to such an interesting gentleman. Such a conversationalist!" Miss Bingley exchanged sly smiles with her sister.

There was no way Elizabeth could respond to this latest sally without revealing how the betrothal had ended, thus providing more fodder for Miss Bingley's conversational canons. Damn the woman!

Elizabeth carefully set down her fork. "Actually, Mr. Collins and I ended our engagement while I was visiting Kent." Her eyes remained focused on the plate before her.

"You did?" Miss Bingley looked as if she had received an early Christmas present. "I am grieved to hear of it. What a shame you did not learn of the *size* of your incompatibility before the engagement."

Darcy gripped the edge of the table to prevent himself from saying anything rash. Collins's rejection had nothing to do with the size of Elizabeth's dowry, but seeing her pale face, he knew the accusation still stung. He waited for her to respond, but she kept her chin down and her lips tightly pursed. Perhaps Elizabeth preferred to allow Caroline Bingley's assumption rather than revealing the truth.

Anger grew behind Darcy's eyes like a headache, pressing and demanding. Caroline Bingley was hurting Elizabeth, threatening her. Surely he could do something to wipe that smug expression off the woman's face!

As a child, Darcy had sometimes been accused of gaining enjoyment by shocking other people. Perhaps it had to do with the time he brought a duck into his mother's bedchamber, or when he demonstrated to his father his newfound talent for jumping off the back of a moving horse. As he had grown, he had lost his taste for such antics, particularly after his mother's death.

But apparently some of that spirit remained buried inside him.

He carefully monitored Miss Bingley's movements from the corner of his eye. She was reaching for her glass of wine. Perfect.

Darcy gave a calculated laugh. "Elizabeth is entirely too circumspect to share with you the entirety of the events in Kent, Miss Bingley." All eyes turned to him as he patted Elizabeth's hand where it rested on the table. "There is no shame in telling the truth now, darling." At this endearment, Elizabeth's head whipped in his direction, her expression bewildered. He turned his gaze back to Miss Bingley. "But the truth is, she has graciously accepted my offer of marriage."

Chapter 7

Miss Bingley coughed and spewed out her mouthful of wine all over the white tablecloth. Perfect timing, Darcy congratulated himself. Although the maid who washed the linens might not think so…

Next to his sister, Bingley's expression had gone from shocked to delighted in two seconds. He thumped her on the back as she coughed, and her eyes watered.

Miss Jane Bennet seemed positively alarmed, her gaze fixed on her sister. Elizabeth regarded Darcy with wide, almost panicked eyes, a deep blush covering her cheeks. He grasped her hand in his—and gave her a besotted smile, silently willing her to play along.

"I know that the declaration of my feelings came as something of a shock to you," he said to her.

"Tha—" Elizabeth cleared her throat. "That is quite an understatement, Mis-my dear." Her voice was quite strangled. Next to her sister, Jane Bennet was shaking, her mouth covered with a handkerchief. Was she laughing? "You took me completely by surprise. In fact, I have not yet recovered from the shock." Elizabeth's eyes held a spark of mischief that suggested she appreciated the humor of the situation.

Darcy gave an inward sigh of relief that she was not taking offense at his high-handedness. But did she understand the unexpected announcement was a result of his genuine passion for her? Or did she simply believe it was a joke—as before, with Collins? He was well aware how far he had to go before convincing her of his worthiness as a husband.

Charles's efforts seemed to make Miss Bingley's plight worse rather than better; her face had actually taken on a bluish tinge, but her brother took no notice. "Congratulations, Darcy!" The man's face was wreathed in smiles. "You are a sly fellow. I had no idea you were interested in Miss Elizabeth!"

Mrs. Hurst seemed to be having some difficulty breathing and was fanning herself vigorously. The announcement had caused Mr. Hurst to pause in his attention to his meat, but now he attacked it with renewed interest.

Elizabeth had tilted her head downward and covered her smile with her free hand. But she glanced up at him through a veil of lashes. The effect was simultaneously bashful and incredibly alluring. Darcy would swear the blood in his veins pumped faster. His heart thudded as if he were running a race. A wildly inappropriate and almost irresistible need to kiss her seized him.

"Yes, pray tell us when you first conceived of your interest in me." Elizabeth no doubt intended the words to be teasing, but accompanied by such enticing glances, they had quite a different effect on Darcy.

Slowing his breathing, Darcy willed his heart to cease its erratic beat. But her faint rosewater scent teased his nose. The touch of her hand…the soft and silky feel of her skin... He could barely reign in his passions when she was on the other side of the room. How was he to contain them when her skin touched his?

He swallowed. "It is difficult to say. It has been coming on so gradually. But perhaps it was your muddy petticoat." Elizabeth's eyes danced with amusement. "It spoke so well of your concern for your sister."

"You told me you would not like Georgiana to emulate such an example." Miss Bingley had unfortunately recovered her powers of speech. Somehow she conveyed a sneer just by looking at Elizabeth.

Naturally the woman would remember that particular offhand comment of his! Darcy thought furiously how to respond. "I merely meant that Georgiana is not a strong walker and would not have enjoyed such a walk as well as Elizabeth." He noticed a corner of Elizabeth's mouth curve up. Did she suspect the truth?

"And perhaps Mr. Collins is not fond of long walks. Was that the difficulty which brought you to the position of having two different fiancés in one week?" Miss Bingley arched an eyebrow at Elizabeth.

Elizabeth raised her eyes to meet the other woman's, but Darcy noticed her flush. "Mr. Collins and I quickly realized we could not make each other happy."

"And Mr. Darcy was conveniently available." Miss Bingley's voice dripped with sarcasm.

Was she implying that Elizabeth had somehow tricked him into a betrothal? If only she knew how far that was from the truth! Darcy considered how he might convey that information without betraying his loathing for Miss Bingley.

"I could not have been happier that Elizabeth accepted me." He smiled at Elizabeth as he spoke, wishing she did not appear faintly puzzled. "I thought I had lost my opportunity when she was betrothed to Mr. Collins." Elizabeth regarded him steadily, a little crease between her brows.

"Indeed?" Miss Bingley stared at their intertwined hands. "I am all astonishment."

Too low for anyone else to hear, Elizabeth murmured, "As am I." But when Darcy's eyes sought hers, they were focused on her plate.

He sighed, wishing he knew how she truly felt about him. He could only hope the expression of those feelings would not take the form of packing for Longbourn.

***

The women withdrew while the men finished their meal with a glass of port. In theory, the ladies would discuss matters of fashion and running a household while the men would converse on weighty topics such as war and politics. In practice, Elizabeth sat on one side of the drawing room with Jane while Miss Bingley and Mrs. Hurst sat on the other, speaking in outraged tones and giving Elizabeth sly looks. She could only imagine what the other women were saying about her.

"Lizzy?" Jane's voice drew Elizabeth's attention back to her sister. "You truly had no idea Mr. Darcy admires you?"

Elizabeth laughed but kept her voice low as she replied, "As I said before, he does *not* admire me. That announcement was simply a joke on his part." *I just do not know whether it was at my expense or Miss Bingley's.*

Jane shook her head slowly. "I do not believe so. I have noticed before how he regards you."

"That is ridiculous!" Jane raised her eyebrows at Elizabeth's tone, and she lowered her voice. "If he did have feelings for me, why would he not have declared himself? Why this charade of having already proposed to me? It makes no sense!"

"He did say something similar to Mr. Collins," Jane observed.

"Oh, Jane," Elizabeth gave her a sweet smile, "You are forever a romantic. But I am the last woman Mr. Darcy would consider marrying."

Jane bit her lip. "If that is the case, he should not toy with you."

"I daresay he does not see it that way," Elizabeth responded. "He is simply amusing himself."

"It is a strange topic for a jest."

"Indeed." Elizabeth was about to venture another opinion about their host, but at that moment, the door opened, and the gentlemen filed in: Mr. Bingley, followed by Mr. Hurst and Mr. Darcy, whose eyes immediately sought hers.

His expression could best be described as anxious. Was he concerned she would reveal his deception at this late hour? He crossed the room in a few strides and took the chair next to hers. Such behavior would have surprised her, but she supposed it was in keeping with his desire to play the part of the attentive fiancé.

Mr. Hurst immediately took himself to the room's fainting couch, with which he was already intimately acquainted, having spent many hours in peaceful slumber there. Mr. Bingley surveyed the room's occupants. "Who would care to join me for a few hands of whist?"

Jane stood at once, and Mrs. Hurst expressed her delight with the scheme. They set up a hand at a table in the corner, eventually persuading Miss Bingley to join them. Elizabeth admired how neatly Mr. Bingley had diverted the others and wondered if Mr. Darcy had asked it of his friend.

Now that they enjoyed relative privacy, Mr. Darcy leaned forward, resting his arms on his thighs, but made no move to touch her. "So, Miss Bennet, how angry are you with me?"

"Angry?" she echoed.

"I just declared a betrothal you never agreed to. Certainly, you are entitled to some indignation."

"I must confess to some degree of surprise. Why did you see fit to reveal our supposed attachment in such a manner?" She arched an eyebrow at him.

"I…to own the truth, Miss Bingley's attacks upon your character angered me greatly. She had no right to make such unjust accusations." His face red, he fixed his gaze on his shoes.

This answer was unexpected, and Elizabeth took a moment to respond. "And you decided an engagement with me was the best way to punish Miss Bingley?"

"No! I-I had…I wished to protect you from her. She has ever been your critic." He dragged a hand through his dark hair. "She is unfair and spiteful. I fear I let my anger rule me. I knew an engagement with me was an unassailable reason for discontinuing your engagement with Mr. Collins."

Elizabeth turned the words over in her mind again, certain she could not have correctly grasped their import. Mr. Darcy wished to *protect* her? Was she awake, or had she slipped into some kind of dream world?

Mr. Darcy was still speaking. "...But I fear that my impulsive words may have placed you in a more difficult and awkward position. I apologize."

His expression was so desolate Elizabeth felt the need to comfort him. "I am certain no damage was done, although Miss Bingley may wonder why no wedding takes place."

"You may feel free to throw me over at your leisure." His lighthearted tone was at odds with the pained expression on his face.

"I can hardly jilt you if no engagement exists, sir!"

He grimaced. "I suppose not. However, I would prefer not to reveal the truth at once. If Miss Bingley acts too triumphant, I might be tempted to strangle her."

Elizabeth covered her smile with her hand. "Well, in the interests of preventing future homicide, I would be loath to reveal anything."

"You are generosity itself." He gave her a conspiratorial smile that took her breath away. He really was quite a handsome man. Elizabeth quickly cast about for a different topic of conversation.

"Er...what about your sister? She may find our sudden betrothal perplexing."

He frowned. "I will discuss the situation with her."

Elizabeth nodded. "Very well, I shall strive to be an agreeable false fiancée to you."

Mr. Darcy's frown deepened. "Not false, merely...temporary."

"If you wish." Elizabeth shrugged. The man was as much of a mystery as always.

***

"I never thought I would see it!"

This had to be the third time Bingley had said those words, but Darcy did not care. Tonight, nothing could dim his high spirits. Elizabeth might regard the "engagement" as temporary, but he could not help viewing it as a step closer to winning her regard. Mr. Hurst and the female guests had retired to their bedchambers, leaving Darcy and Bingley with their first true opportunity to talk alone since the "announcement."

"Darcy of Pemberley marrying a girl from the country! The *ton* will be abuzz with gossip for—well, at least days."

Darcy sighed and sank another ball into a corner pocket of the billiard table. He knew he should reveal the truth to his friend, but he hated to admit how he had dissembled or that the impetus for the deception was anger at Bingley's sister. In addition, truth be told, he enjoyed imagining Elizabeth as his fiancée, even if it was an illusion. Admitting the truth would strip away the comforting illusion. On the other hand, if he said nothing, perhaps he could convince Elizabeth to make the engagement permanent.

"Perhaps. We have not yet made the news public."

Bingley swallowed more brandy as he watched Darcy set up another shot. "Do not mistake me, my friend. I believe you have made a marvelous choice. I am simply astounded. Astonished. Flummoxed." Perhaps Bingley had consumed a sufficient amount of brandy for the night.

Darcy sank two balls into another pocket, but Bingley did not react; the other man's eyes were not focused on the billiard table but were fixed rather glassily on a painting on the opposite wall. Yes, indeed, enough brandy.

Darcy straightened and chalked his cue. "I was a bit astonished at my own feelings, to own the truth." What a relief to confide in someone after concealing his sentiments and intentions for so long!

"I can imagine!" Bingley's voice had grown louder as the night progressed; just as well the other guests had retired. "I always thought you would marry the daughter of an earl or some such." He waved his hand airily.

Darcy snorted. "I had enough of those types of women after my first Season in Town."

Bingley nodded rather too vigorously and then grabbed the edge of the billiard table to keep from listing to the side. Perhaps it was time for them to quit for the night. "They are not to my taste either," Bingley opined.

Darcy grunted an assent as he leaned over the table, concentrating on the remaining two balls. If he cleared the table, they could both retire. After announcing the engagement, he had been filled with a kind of agitated energy. But—whether it was the brandy or the late hour— he now thought he might be capable of sleep.

"Do you know another reason I am pleased about your betrothal?" Bingley continued without awaiting a reply from Darcy. "Because your engagement to Miss Elizabeth Bennet will make it easier for me to propose to Miss Jane Bennet." Bingley waved his empty brandy glass emphatically. "Caroline will still object, but if the family is good enough for you, they are certainly good enough for me!"

"Are you considering offering for her?" Darcy asked. One of the balls shot into a side pocket.

"I believe I shall." Bingley swayed a bit and leaned on the billiard table for balance. "You and Caroline were not sure of her feelings, but I think she does like *me*—and not because her mother likes my fortune!"

Darcy looked up from the table. "For what it is worth, I am convinced I was mistaken about her regard for you."

"You were?" Bingley blinked owlishly at his friend. "Well, good! I might even offer tomorrow. Love is in the air and all that." Bingley laughed as he made a twirling motion with his finger.

Bingley might not notice if they failed to end the game, but Darcy felt compelled by honor to finish according to the rules. He sank the last ball. "That is the game," Darcy informed his friend.

Bingley stared in bewilderment at the now-empty table. "Did I win?"

Darcy suppressed a laugh and clasped his friend's shoulder. "You acquitted yourself well, but now it is time for bed."

He racked his cue and Bingley's, then gestured for his friend to precede him out the door. Bingley was steadier on his feet than Darcy had expected. Then Bingley bumped against the wall, and Darcy was forced to revise his opinion of his friend's sobriety. He put a hand under Bingley's elbow and led him toward the stairs.

"Have you ever noticed Jane's hair? It is like sunshine come to earth! She is such an angel." Bingley rambled on as they slowly stumbled across the marble of the front hallway. "Do you believe she likes me? I have never tried to kiss her—"

"I should think not!" Darcy exclaimed. He kept one hand on the banister and one on Bingley's arm as they ascended the stairs.

"But sometimes I think she might let me. And then other times…her face is so serene." Bingley's mumbling was so soft, Darcy was not sure if he was expected to respond. "It is very restful, but how do I know if she cares for me?"

Darcy was tempted to laugh. "Good God, she lights up like a candle when you enter the room!"

Bingley stopped on the uppermost step, swaying slightly. Alarmed, Darcy tugged his friend away from the top of the stairs and toward the guest wing. "She does?" A silly smile lit Bingley's face.

Darcy rolled his eyes. "Indeed. It is glaringly obvious to everyone."

"Except me apparently." Bingley actually giggled. He leaned close to Darcy, breathing brandy into his face. "Do you really think so?"

"I do." Darcy kept his face straight, giving his words the solemnity Bingley deserved.

"Good! I will propose tomorrow!" Bingley turned and strode rapidly toward the bedchambers. Wanting to ensure that his friend would make it to his bed, Darcy hastened to follow.

He intervened before Bingley inadvertently opened the door to his sister's bedchamber and steered his friend to his own door. Once Bingley was inside his room, Darcy had discharged his duty and could seek his own room.

His steps now took him toward the family wing of the house, boot heels tapping on the wooden floor. He passed the door to Georgiana's room. After the other ladies had retired for the night, Darcy had visited his sister, pleased to learn that her headache had abated.

He had acquainted her with the events of the evening, confessing his feelings for Elizabeth, which his perceptive sister had already guessed. In fact, he had told Georgiana nearly everything—save the depth of his physical desire for his "fiancée." It had been such a relief to confess everything, and the siblings had talked and laughed for quite some time. Georgiana had expressed delight at the idea of Elizabeth becoming her future sister.

Now Darcy was approaching Elizabeth's door. He had indulged himself by putting Elizabeth's bedchamber in the family wing—where she would be closer to his room—rather than the guest wing. Fortunately, he been capable of resisting his mad desire to ensconce her in the chambers for the lady of Pemberley; it would have given rise to too many questions—not the least of which from Elizabeth herself.

Unfortunately, placing Elizabeth *alone* in the family wing would have looked suspicious, so he had Mrs. Reynolds situate Jane Bennet in the adjacent bedchamber, which shared a sitting room with Elizabeth's room.

Bingley's words about kissing Jane Bennet came back to Darcy, eliciting a chuckle. It would be quite scandalous if Bingley had kissed his beloved before their engagement. After an official engagement, couples enjoyed greater leeway in their behavior.

Darcy stumbled and nearly fell.

Everyone at Pemberley believes I am engaged to Elizabeth.

I could kiss her.

Why had this not occurred to him before? Memories of her lips occupied his thoughts: the exact dark pinkish red shade of her lips, the shape—with the lower lip slightly fuller than the top. Perfect. He could bend down…she would tilt her head up…her lips would part slightly… revealing a glimpse of her delicate pink tongue.

What was that noise? Oh, he had groaned aloud. And now his body was responding to this fantasy. He was fortunate no one was awake to see him. As his skin grew overheated and his clothing felt too tight for his body, he had come to a dead stop in the middle of the hallway. He leaned against the wall for stability, the plaster cooling his skin.

But Elizabeth does not consider herself betrothed to me. Why would she permit a kiss?

The thought threw cold water on his ardor.

She had appeared so puzzled when he had explained himself in the drawing room. He had deliberately avoided speaking of his true feelings; she was not ready for such a declaration. Instead, she believed his motives to be purely altruistic, and he knew it would not be long before she cried off. If he wished to convince her of his sincere devotion, he would need to do so quickly.

That would require he make an effort to court her despite their supposed engagement. Darcy rubbed his face with his hands. How had he become caught up in this situation? His life had been straightforward and orderly. Then he had met Elizabeth Bennet, and ever since…it was like attempting to steer a ship on the high seas during a storm. But she was worth it.

With a smile on his lips, Darcy pushed away from the wall and took a few more steps down the hall. Hopefully tomorrow, he would have an opportunity to speak with Elizabeth alone. Perhaps he could manufacture a "chance" meeting…

As he reached the door to Elizabeth's room, Darcy could not help reaching out to touch the smooth oak, dreaming about the woman within.

There were faint sounds from within the bedchamber. Was someone talking? Darcy pressed his ear against the door. Yes, Elizabeth's voice, too low for him to discern any words. Who could she be speaking with at this time of night? Was her sister visiting? But he heard no other voices. Was she sick, in the grip of feverish delusions?

The thought made him want to burst into her room, but he could not. Even with a chaperone, it would be awkward, but alone, in the middle of the night? It was unthinkable.

The sound of Elizabeth's voice tapered off, and Darcy stepped away from the door, preparing to return to his room. Perhaps Elizabeth simply talked in her sleep. Georgiana occasionally did so.

But then —a shrill scream emanated from her room, piercing the night. Without hesitating, Darcy slammed open the door and raced into Elizabeth's room.

Chapter 8

Elizabeth had been enjoying a stroll with her father in the gardens at Pemberley. It seemed the most natural thing in the world. Papa was talking about Mr. Darcy's puzzling behavior and reminding her that he had earlier seemed so unpleasant and difficult.

Before Elizabeth could reply, and without warning, her father fell forward, his eyes open, staring at her with a pleading, desperate look on his face. She tried to catch him in her arms and break his fall but could not hold his weight long enough to even slow his descent. He crumpled to the ground. She screamed.

"Elizabeth!"

Papa hit the stone pathway with a sickening thud. She screamed again.

"Elizabeth!"

She opened her eyes. She was sitting up in bed, wearing her linen nightgown. Relief flooded her: she was at Pemberley, and it had been a dream. The room was swathed in shadows, but there was dim moonlight filtering in through the curtains. Enough that she could see Mr. Darcy crouching at her bedside.

"Mr. Darcy!" Instinctively, Elizabeth pulled up the coverlet to conceal the front of her nightgown. Of course, the garment covered her from neck to toe, but she still felt exposed; no man had ever before seen her in her night clothing, save her father.

In reaction, Mr. Darcy stood and stumbled away from her bedside. "Forgive me, Miss Bennet." He ran a trembling hand through his hair, further disheveling it. "I heard a scream. I could not…I believed…I feared you were in some danger."

Was he blushing? It was difficult to tell in the meager light, but Elizabeth thought she detected a hint of color in his cheeks. At least she was not the only one embarrassed by the circumstances.

"I screamed?" She was certain her face must be bright red.

Mr. Darcy nodded. "I was out in the corridor, and I heard...perhaps you had a nightmare?"

Thank goodness, Jane was a deep sleeper! Although it would be far less embarrassing to have her sister in her bedchamber. Still, Elizabeth was grateful not to be alone at the moment. "Yes, I..." Reaching up to her cheek, she felt moisture on her fingertips. Must she cry before Mr. Darcy—again?

The dream was still vivid in her mind; her body trembled, and her heart raced. The nightmare must have held her in its thrall for some time. She rubbed her eyes as if she could dispel the memories. "It was very unpleasant."

Mr. Darcy's eyes were sympathetic. "Would you like to talk about it?"

Her hands, resting on top of the coverlet, shook violently. Her mind insisted on recalling again and again that moment when her father fell forward into her hands, the stricken look on his face. God forbid such a thing would ever happen in reality! "No, I...I think it would be better to attempt to forget."

"Yes, yes, of course." He glanced about the room as if hoping the means to forget would present itself. "Perhaps a book or a glass of wine would help you fall back to sleep?"

Elizabeth considered for a moment, trying to discreetly wipe the tears away with her fingertips. "I am prone to nightmares. If I sleep immediately, I may fall into another one right away. If I were at home—" She stopped herself. This was not Longbourn. Mr. Darcy was her host, and it was mortifying enough that he had heard her scream. She should trouble him no more.

"Yes?" he prompted.

"It is nothing. I should allow you to return to your room."

Mr. Darcy took her hand, gently and carefully engulfing it in his. "I beg you, tell me how I may be of assistance."

Elizabeth sighed. Despite the impropriety, he clearly would not leave her room until she was in improved spirits. "At home, I walk the corridors for a time. When I am weary enough, then I return to bed. This always ensures a dreamless sleep."

Mr. Darcy tugged on Elizabeth's hand, pulling her forward to the edge of her bed. "Come, there are miles of corridors in Pemberley. Some are little used even during the day."

Elizabeth perched on the edge of her bed but pulled her hand back. "I can hardly wander the halls in your company, sir. You should not even be in my room. Thank goodness no one is awake!"

Mr. Darcy looked stricken, dropping her hand immediately. "I apologize, Eliz—Miss Bennet. I know my behavior was precipitous and do not want to impose—"

He should not regret his concern for her. "No," Elizabeth held up her hand, "I appreciate—very much— your anxiety for my well-being. I am simply concerned that gossip might attach to our reputations. But please believe that you have my trust."

His breath caught, as if he could not believe his good fortune. He raised her hand to his lips, gently brushing them over the back. "Your trust is…a precious gift." Turning her hand over, he delicately kissed the inside of her palm.

Elizabeth shivered. Her palm appeared to be directly connected to her spine so that these delicious tremors of sensation spread throughout her body. She found herself staring at his dark, lustrous hair, wondering how it would feel. Was it as soft as it looked? How would his cheek feel under her fingertips, with the roughness of his beard stubble?

My heavens! Why was she having such thoughts about *Mr. Darcy*?

How did he spur such imaginings? And why was he behaving in such an uncharacteristic manner? First, he declares they are engaged, and now he charges into her room and kisses her palm. What was the man about?

"Certainly, you may roam the halls of Pemberley at your leisure. I need not accompany you." His smile was half-hearted.

Elizabeth found herself loath to disappoint him. "I believe I *shall* roam the halls." His eyes narrowed slightly as she spoke. "And, if I should encounter the master of the house while roaming, well, who would be surprised?"

"I do not need—"

"I would be grateful for the company," she said quickly—and quite accurately. She was coming to believe she needed to know Mr. Darcy better. Perhaps a quiet, uninterrupted talk would solve some of the mysteries he presented.

"Ah, well, I would not wish disappoint you." Mr. Darcy's voice was light, but his eyes were very dark and wide as they fixed on her face—as if she held all the secrets of the universe.

"And after all, we are allowed some liberties now that we are engaged." She gave him a mischievous smile, but the look she received in return was dark and serious.

"Indeed." He took a deep breath and then looked about the room. "Have you a dressing gown?"

She nodded, gesturing to a hook in the closet. He fetched the garment and held it up for her the way a maid might, which did not prevent her face from heating as she slid out from under the coverlet. It was quite indecent for Mr. Darcy to see her in her nightclothes. However, he studiously stared at the fireplace as she shrugged her arms into the dressing gown and buttoned up the front.

More at ease, Elizabeth turned to face Mr. Darcy, murmuring her thanks for his assistance. For the first time, she was aware that the master of Pemberley was somewhat less than formally attired. He still wore his breeches and boots but had discarded his coat and waistcoat.

Even his cravat was missing, and his shirt collar was open, revealing his neck. Naturally, Elizabeth had never before seen this part of his body, and the effect was somewhat…disquieting. Unbidden, her eyes were drawn to forbidden territory, the pale column of his throat. He was so much more open, more approachable…more…vulnerable.

Stop staring! she ordered herself sternly. *You knew he possessed a neck!*

But in truth, seeing it was a different matter—almost as if she were viewing him naked. *Why does he stand so close?* The heat radiating from his skin seemed to warm her as well, increasing her awareness of his body.

Mr. Darcy cleared his throat, now staring determinedly at a far corner of the room, and took a step back from her. Oh, Good Lord, had her body started swaying toward his? Elizabeth hastily straightened her spine, looking toward the door, certain her blush must extend all the way to her feet. Had he noticed her staring at his throat? What must he think of her?

She now deeply regretted suggesting that he accompany her as she walked. Perhaps she could feign a twisted ankle…or a sudden attack of apoplexy. No, it would not do. She simply must bear up and follow through despite her bad judgment. Their walk could be of short duration.

With renewed resolve, Elizabeth managed a smile, which Mr. Darcy returned tentatively. He held out his arm, and she took it, just as if they were embarking on a stroll through the garden or an entrance to a ball. Given their attire, the effect was quite absurd.

With his free hand, Mr. Darcy picked up a lit candle from her bedside table, then led her down the hallway and to the grand staircase. Elizabeth would have preferred the back stairs, or even the servants' staircase, but she held her head high as she descended the marble expanse in nothing but a dressing gown. She would not let Mr. Darcy know she suffered a moment's discomfort. Nonetheless, she was grateful that no one was about to notice them.

"Where would you like to explore?" Mr. Darcy inquired as they reached the black-and-white floor of the front hall. "Pemberley is full of many interesting rooms, but my goal is to find a restful location for you."

Elizabeth assumed an air of speculative contemplation. "Then I suppose we should avoid the torture chamber in the dungeon."

Mr. Darcy laughed, a hearty, rippling sound she had never heard before. "Yes, and the room where my family preserves the skulls of those who have dared to cross us."

Elizabeth chuckled. "No, the Darcy family would never be so crass as to preserve such gruesome trophies. Lady Catherine, however…"

Mr. Darcy grimaced. "Indeed. Since we speak of family history, perhaps you would like to see the gallery. I would show you the portraits of my mother and father."

"Oh, yes!" Elizabeth had no need to feign enthusiasm. "I have not visited that room."

Mr. Darcy's easy smile suggested he was pleased by her interest. He led her through a series of grand, dimly lit rooms until they arrived at the gallery. It boasted a row of tall windows on one side and an impressive array of family portraits on the other. Moonlight streaming through the windows cast some paintings in a silvery glow while others were swathed in shadow.

Mr. Darcy used the candle from Elizabeth's room to ignite the wall sconces until the room positively blazed with light. The warm light from the candles was reflected off hundreds of crystals hanging from the three chandeliers positioned along the gallery's ceiling. The light on the portraits flickered irregularly—making the people in them seem to move and dance as if they were alive. The effect was entirely magical.

"It is a lovely room," she breathed.

"I thank you," Mr. Darcy said. His voice was level, but a spark in his eyes hinted that her compliment mattered to him, although she could not imagine why. Surely many people more important than Elizabeth Bennet had approved of Pemberley.

It was time to focus on a neutral subject. Elizabeth turned to the first portrait, a full-length painting of a man in Elizabethan garb. "Which ancestor is this?"

"Robert Darcy," Mr. Darcy responded. "In many ways, the first of the line."

"You said the Pemberley library was the work of many generations. How old is the building?"

"*This* Pemberley is not so old, but there was a much older structure built during the Tudor period. It burned down, unfortunately. So my grandfather, Edward Darcy, tore down the ruins and built the structure you see today. However, the old library escaped the fire, so the collection survived intact."

"Thank goodness," Elizabeth breathed. Mr. Darcy nodded in agreement. Yes, he would appreciate how awful the loss of books would be.

"When was the first building constructed?" she asked.

"The original structure was begun in…." As Mr. Darcy's words washed over her, Elizabeth watched him—his mouth, his hands, his very body told her of his passion for the subject and for his ancestral home. It was more than familial pride that shone through his words but also the sense of tradition and stewardship for the families in his care. She could not remain unaffected.

She asked more questions, and he answered, eager to discuss Pemberley without the reticence that so often characterized him. How fortunate she had visited Pemberley and viewed this passion firsthand! If only she could be part of that tradition. Remain part of his life.

Wait! Why had she thought that?

No, it was absurd. She was grateful for his kindness toward her. Certainly, her feelings had undergone a shift since she realized he did not disapprove of her, but when she departed from Pemberley, she would most likely never seem him again—except perhaps if he visited Netherfield.

Of course, I do not yearn to be part of his life.

This is Mr. Darcy, *after all.*

Yet compassion lit his face as he described a flood that had disrupted the lives of some Pemberley tenants twenty-five years ago. Every part of his face was alive. His hands moved back and forth as he described changes to the property. He was so different from the dour, difficult man who had arrived at the Meryton Assembly! If this man had arrived, she would have…

Elizabeth found herself a little shocked at her thoughts.

If Mr. Darcy had shown this intelligence and passion and openness at their first meeting, she would have eagerly sought out his company. She would have wished to converse with him and dance with him. In fact, her behavior might have closely resembled Jane's with Mr. Bingley.

The thought left her breathless.

"Eliz-Miss Bennet?"

Elizabeth pulled herself from her reverie, blinking at Mr. Darcy, who was standing far closer than she remembered. And this was the second time he had almost called her by her Christian name. What did that mean?

"Are you quite well?" His forehead was creased with worry.

"Yes, I assure you," she said quickly.

"You appear a little pale. Perhaps some wine? I have some in my study." His eyes scanned her face.

Sharing the gallery with him unchaperoned and in her dressing gown was quite overwhelming enough. Elizabeth could not imagine venturing into the intimacy of his study. "That is not necessary."

Mr. Darcy took a step back and looked away, his hands worrying the edges of his cuffs. "I am afraid I must have bored you. I am certain you did not need so much detail about the history of Pemberley."

"Not at all," she reassured him.

He frowned. "I am well aware that not everyone finds Pemberley as fascinating as I do."

"I found the history very interesting. Particularly when you tell it."

Oh, would he take that the wrong way and believe I am flirting with him?

Gracious, am *I flirting with him?*

But apparently Mr. Darcy's thoughts were running in quite a different direction. "I hope you find Pemberley to your liking." There was an unexpected strain in his voice.

"I do, very much. I imagine few would dislike it." Had they not already had this conversation? Why did her approval mean so much to him?

"It is important to me that you have a pleasant stay."

Why? Is he that concerned about my state of mind after Mr. Collins's rejection?

Casting about for a new topic of conversation, she asked, "Where are the portraits of your parents?"

"Here." Mr. Darcy guided her down the gallery with a hand at the small of her back. "This is my mother, and that is my father."

The portraits were splendidly done and very lifelike. "You resemble your father very much."

Mr. Darcy shrugged and colored slightly. "I can only strive to be as good a man. He was dearly beloved here."

"Your mother was very beautiful," Elizabeth said. "How old were you when she passed away?"

"Twelve." Mr. Darcy hesitated. "She was a wonderful mother and an able mistress for Pemberley. Finding her replacement has not been an easy task."

"I would imagine," Elizabeth murmured. What did he mean by that? Did he seek to warn her off from any dreams she might have of becoming mistress of Pemberley?

Once again, she realized his eyes were upon her. She shifted uncomfortably, glancing about the room at the windows facing the garden. "The moonlight is quite beautiful."

"Would you like to go out to the terrace?" Mr. Darcy inquired. "It may be bright enough to see something of the garden."

The man always made such unexpected suggestions! She should no longer be surprised. "Oh, ah—" There were many reasons it would be a bad idea, but she seemed unable to articulate a single one.

Mr. Darcy's head dropped slightly. "Although perhaps it is too chilly at this time of night. I should have considered that."

No, she would not allow him to chastise himself on her behalf. And the terrace did tempt her. "Not at all. I would love to view the garden."

Mr. Darcy gave her a long, considering look. Finally, he led her to a set of French doors and ushered her outside.

The air had a bite of night chill but did not make her shiver, and the view was as lovely as Elizabeth had hoped. The moon bathed everything in a silvery light, which made the familiar shapes and sights look otherworldly and foreign. Long shadows were cast by the balcony's balustrade and the potted plants. Frogs or insects of some kind supplied a rhythmic chorus from the trees below.

Elizabeth strolled to the edge of the balcony, delighting in the view of the garden. "The moon is so bright!" she marveled. "It is almost like day." However, the moon's light was cool and blue, not at all like the yellow glow of the sun.

After admiring the garden for a minute, Elizabeth turned and was surprised to see Mr. Darcy standing close, regarding her with a faint smile on his lips. "Am I amusing you?" she asked sportively.

"No." He frowned slightly. "Well, rather, yes. I find your delight in such beauty to be... appealing."

Compelled to look away from his intense gaze, Elizabeth fixed her eyes on a shrub in the garden below. He spoke so directly! This was not the first time she had been startled by such declarations, but feeling completely unequal to making a reply, she fell silent.

***

Darcy was a turmoil of conflicting impulses. The battle of these different instincts must be plain on his face. He longed to touch Elizabeth, feel her skin, thrust his fingers into her hair, trace the delicacy of her eyebrow, or tease the area below her ear. Would she shiver with delight? Would she gasp? Would she permit him to kiss her?

Or would she slap him for his presumption?

His better nature argued against giving into such baser instincts. He clasped his hands together behind his back, hoping to restrain his urges. Forcing his eyes away from her, he focused on the far less alluring beauty of the garden.

His hands wished to touch her without ceasing while his mouth could barely refrain from babbling the truth of his love for her. The longing to confess his feelings to her was even stronger than the desire to touch her. What a relief it would be to unburden himself from those long-held secrets! But he knew he must restrain himself. Unbridled emotion might startle and confuse her.

Worse, she might not return the sentiments.

She might smile politely, express her appreciation for his regard, and decline any interest in him. Reluctant agreement with his impulsive declaration of their betrothal hardly constituted a declaration of affection—or even tolerance. The thought froze his blood and stopped the words on his tongue.

The impulse to speak and the need to restrain his speech warred within him, rendering him mute. After a long pause, Elizabeth turned back to rest her hands on the weathered stone of the balustrade. He could think of nothing to say, but like a lodestone, she continued to pull his gaze.

Elizabeth's dark hair was a glorious tumble cascading down her back. The moonlight shimmered off the curls with every movement, mesmerizing him. If only he could reach out a finger and touch even one curl. Would it be as silky smooth and soft as it appeared? He resented the necessity that she would pin her hair up again in the morning.

Elizabeth shot him a sidelong glance. Had he groaned aloud? Damnation! She would think him the worst kind of libertine! Darcy clamped his mouth shut, pressing his lips together to prevent future self-betrayals.

She pushed herself off the balustrade and stood, arms crossed, her gaze now turned inward. "You have been most gracious with your hospitality, but we must not trespass upon your kindness much longer. We should fix our departure in the next few days."

So soon!

Had his inappropriate behavior frightened her into a precipitous departure? "I am pleased to have you as my guests," he murmured. "You need not worry you are overstaying your welcome."

She gave a slight shake of her head. "I cannot delay the inevitable. I must go home and tell my parents the truth about Mr. Collins eventually." Briefly, her lips twisted into an unhappy grimace.

Sudden tension stiffened his entire body. "I wish I could do more to help. You have been placed in a difficult position through no fault of your own." He perceived an opportunity and knew he must chance it. He took a deep breath. "Perhaps it would help to extend our temporary engagement into Hertfordshire."

Elizabeth grew very still, staring at the garden. "You have done so much already." Her tone of finality suggested she thought he had done quite enough.

Was she angry over his declaration of their engagement? Darcy's stomach turned to lead. So much for his hopes of a real betrothal; she did not wish to be associated with him at all. "I see."

Her brow creased, and her eyes darted toward his face. "When you were at Netherfield, I confess, I did not speak very highly of you."

Darcy chuckled mirthlessly. "Why should you? I did not acquit myself well."

"It was not well done of me at all," she insisted. "But now the people of Meryton will find it hard to credit any talk of a sudden engagement."

"They will disbelieve you?" Darcy's eyebrows climbed up to his hairline.

"To speak frankly, I am not the sort of woman anyone would expect you to marry. I have no fortune or family name to boast of. I am—as many remind me—too outspoken. And while I may be tolerably pretty, it hardly compensates for—"

"Enough!" Darcy would not hear one more word. He grabbed her shoulders and forced her to look him in the eye. "Do not disparage yourself this way. Fortune and family connections mean nothing to me. You are an intelligent, vivacious, well-spoken, accomplished young woman. And so lovely it takes my breath away."

Elizabeth's eyes were wide with shock. In a remote corner of his mind, Darcy was aware that he was revealing too much, that he had forgotten his resolve to moderate his speech, but the rest of him was long past caring.

"*Any* man would be fortunate, indeed, to call you his," he finished, softening his voice.

Elizabeth watched him in perplexity, her lips slightly parted—so beautiful, so enticing, it broke his heart. Everything about her called to him.

He could resist no longer.

He pulled her toward him until no space separated them—until their bodies were touching. And he kissed her.

At first, he simply brushed his lips lightly against hers. His heart threatened to pound itself out of his ribs. How would she react? He pulled back a little to evaluate her reaction. Her eyes were half closed, un-focused as she glanced up at him, but she did not seem to take offense at his actions.

Emboldened by this tacit permission, Darcy bent his head to her lips once more. This time, he took possession of her mouth, pressing his lips firmly against hers and demanding entry with his tongue. Her lips parted with a little gasp, allowing him to explore every hidden corner, tasting the distinctive flavor of Elizabeth. He moaned, pulling her closer to him as his tongue sought deeper access.

Elizabeth's lips pressed back against his, and her tongue tangled with his in an erotic dance. *She is kissing me!* The realization emboldened Darcy, giving free rein to his hands, which moved about—pressing into her waist and caressing her back. Her arms tentatively embraced his waist; Darcy's spirits soared. She would not behave in such a way if she did not have some feelings for him.

Plunging fingers into her hair, he stroked the silken strands. One hand descended to discover the tender skin at the nape of her neck, stroking it, savoring the softness of bare skin. He lowered his hand further to caress the delicate skin of her shoulder. Only a little lower, and he could feel her breast…

What am I thinking?

Appalled at how far he had gone, Darcy pulled away abruptly, steadying Elizabeth as she stumbled after the sudden loss of his support. Once she was balanced, Darcy dropped his hand as if her skin burned and stepped back. Trembling hands rubbed his face. Passionate kisses had not been any part of his careful plan to woo her. Why had he acted so precipitously? Had he scared her off?

"Elizabeth…Miss Bennet…I pray you, forgive me. I did not intend…" He dared not glance in her direction and view the condemnation in her eyes, her horror at his actions. What if she demanded to return to Longbourn immediately?

When she did not reply at once, Darcy chanced a glance in her direction. Her gaze was moving between a spot over his shoulder and his face—as if she did not know where to rest her eyes. Her hand reached up to smooth her hair and fell to her side; then as he watched, she smoothed her hair once more.

He could not possibly ascertain if she was horrified by his actions or if—in some small measure—she possibly shared his passion. Now that he was in better possession of his faculties, he reassured himself that she had not pushed him or struggled to escape his grasp.

"Miss Bennet?" His voice was needy, higher pitched than usual. Finally, she focused her gaze on him. "You have my deepest apologies," he repeated as shame engulfed him again.

"Apologies are unnecessary, Mr. Darcy." He winced at the formality of his name on her lips. Did that mean she intended a polite rejection? "I—" She swallowed. "You may have noticed I was not an unwilling participant." Darcy's breath caught.

A delicate blush colored her cheeks, but her eyes held his, displaying her determination to admit the truth. Finally, she broke the gaze and glanced down. "What must you think of me?"

"Mostly, I am thinking I will be relieved if you are not offended."

"Of course not." Her eyelashes fluttered against her cheek, but she did not look up.

"And I am hoping you might do it again," he admitted. "But only with me," he hastened to add.

"I hope you do not believe I go about kissing other men!" Her eyes darted up to his face, and her pert smile flashed across her lips.

"Indeed not!" But even as Darcy said the words, he wondered if Collins had ever kissed her. Instantly, he was consumed with jealousy. No, he must focus his thoughts on Elizabeth. "I do not want you to think I lured you out here so I could steal a kiss or worse—" She gave a slight shake of the head but said nothing. "I had intended to woo you slowly. Kissing was not part of the plan. But then you look so beautiful and…" Her head made a quick jerk of surprise. He thought she had guessed his purpose already but maybe not.

He dared to step forward, reaching out his hand to touch her cheek with his fingertips. Her eyes closed instantly as if she were savoring his touch. "I have long been wishing for you to be my wife in earnest," he murmured.

Her eyes flew open, regarding him in wide-eyed shock. "But I-you—" she stammered.

He smiled gently. "I hope you do not believe I go about kissing other women in such a way."

She colored and lowered her eyes. The sight was so very alluring that Darcy had to restrain himself from using his other hand to pull her closer to him.

"I would be very honored if you consented to be my wife. For many months you have been the only woman I could imagine standing beside me for the rest of my days."

She looked stunned. "Truly?" He nodded. "Why did you not declare yourself before?"

One corner of his mouth quirked up. "Would you have considered my proposal if I had?"

She gave a rueful chuckle. "Perhaps not." His fingers traced the curve of her neck, and she shivered delicately.

"I would venture to say indeed not. I had hoped that time would change your mind." He continued to gently stroke her neck, and she leaned in to the contact. He should not be touching her thus, but she was so delightfully responsive to his every caress, it could only help his cause. "You need not give me an answer now, but promise me you will think of it."

He held his breath, waiting for her response.

Chapter 9

Silence.

Darcy blew out a breath. The moonlight, her unbound hair, the glow in her eyes—everything—had combined to cast a spell over him, causing him to rush her. He had moved too fast, blast it! She was not prepared for a proposal. He opened his mouth to recall his words before they destroyed this delicate mood.

"I will think about it," Elizabeth whispered.

Thank God! Darcy said a silent prayer. "I would do everything in my power to make you happy." He raised one of her hands to his lips and kissed her fingers softly. Another shiver ran through Elizabeth's body. "We should return inside before the night air makes you sick," he said.

She gave a small smile. "I am actually quite warm." She made no move to return to the house, so Darcy did not move. Perhaps he inched a little closer to her…simply to share with her with more of his warmth.

"There is something I must tell you." Her voice was low, and her eyes fixed on the stone of the terrace.

Silence stretched between them. "Yes?" he finally prompted. Her tone was not promising. Had she already decided against him? Had she been concealing dark secret?

She pulled away from him and leaned against the balustrade; her hand moved restlessly over the weathered stone. "My father…" Her voice cracked, and she cleared her throat. "My father is not well. It is uncertain, but his doctor fears he does not have long to live." Tears were glistening in her eyes, but she blinked them back. "When I was initially disinclined to accept Mr. Collins's offer, my father told me of the doctor's news. No one else in the family knows." She swallowed back a sob.

Darcy experienced a sharp and sudden anger at Mr. Bennet. How dare he put Elizabeth in such a position? Forcing her to accept that repulsive man! But anger was almost immediately tempered by compassion. The master of Longbourn had quite rightly feared for his daughters' future; Collins's offer to Elizabeth must have appeared fortuitous.

Darcy was also relieved to have solved the mystery of why she had accepted the fool's proposal in the first place—and why she had been so devastated at the loss of his regard. The revelation dispelled any doubts he might have harbored about her feelings for Collins.

But then Darcy's heart constricted again. *If she accepted Collins to secure her family's future, why did she not leap at the opportunity to accept me? Certainly, I can fulfill the role just as well—even better! If she hesitates, she must have serious reservations about my character.*

"I see." Darcy was careful to keep his tone neutral.

"Despite his extravagant protestations to the contrary, Mr. Collins did not love me." Now she regarded him earnestly as if begging him to understand—but understand what, exactly?

"Yes," Darcy readily agreed. Collins was incapable of loving anyone, save himself—and possibly Lady Catherine.

"I never told him of my father's illness because it would not have mattered to him why I accepted his offer." Elizabeth spoke quickly.

"Yes," Darcy repeated. Would she refuse him because she feared her motives were not pure? "Elizabeth—"

She held up a hand to forestall his protest. "I tell you this so you understand—" She bit her lip. "I…If I accept your hand, it will *not* be because of my father's illness. With you…I cannot make such a decision for…the wrong reason." Once again, tears were welling up in her eyes.

"Oh, Elizabeth…." He took a step forward so he could stroke her cheek again. Now that he understood her words, Darcy's heart overflowed with love for this woman. She would sacrifice the chance to secure her family's future rather than risk causing him heartache. He vowed that even if she later refused his offer, he would find a way to help the Bennet family.

Her honesty stunned and humbled him. The time had come for him to be wholly honest in return. "Thank you for sharing your confidence with me." His voice was husky with emotion. He clasped one of her hands and kissed it. "And for your candor. Although I can truthfully say I would be happy to have you for whatever reason."

"Perhaps I should accept your offer because of the evenness of your handwriting? Or because I wish to redecorate the mistress's chambers here at Pemberley?" She gave him a cheeky smile that lifted his spirits.

"I have an admission to make as well."

"Oh?" Her face immediately sobered.

Leaning his elbows on the balustrade, he focused on the shadowed garden. "I...er...when I arrived at Longbourn and you were engaged to Mr. Collins...I was unhappy." No, he must be utterly honest. "Truthfully, I was jealous. Until your betrothal, I had not known my own heart—that I was hoping to make you mine." He chanced a quick glance at Elizabeth, but her expression revealed nothing.

His fingers stroked the rough stone. "In my defense, I did not believe you loved him or that he would be a good husband for you." Elizabeth made a sound that could have been a snort. "I wrote to my aunt suggesting she invite you for a visit—with the hopes that it would separate you from Mr. Collins." He risked another look. Her eyes were wide. Was she horrified by his actions?

"It did not occur to me that he would not honor his promise to you," Darcy added hastily. "I never would have caused you such grief. Rather, I believed that acquaintance with my aunt would cause you to change your mind.

Obviously, I did not know about your concerns over your father's health."

Darcy straightened his shoulders and faced Elizabeth, ready to accept her condemnation. Her hand had risen to cover her mouth. Was she concealing her horror at his actions? "I can only beg your forgiveness most abjectly."

Elizabeth said nothing, her lips set in a thin, white line.

Darcy's heart sank. "But I understand if you cannot grant it." Resigned, he stepped past her, seeking the relative safety of the house, but she stayed him with a hand to his sleeve. "You wrote to your aunt about me?" He nodded, unable to discern her expression. Her whole body started to shake; was she cold? She made an odd, strangled noise. "What did you say to her?"

Miss Elizabeth Bennet was sent to this earth to puzzle him, Darcy concluded, but at least she did not appear to be angry. "Nothing but the truth. I wrote that you were an intelligent, vivacious, outspoken young lady."

Laughter bubbled out of Elizabeth's mouth. "No wonder she was alarmed!"

"Indeed." Darcy smiled; it was rather amusing.

"She reacted to me as if I were the whore of Babylon." More chuckles issued forth.

"Indeed not," Darcy said with mock solemnity. "The whore of Babylon would be quite welcome as long as she agreed with Lady Catherine's every utterance."

Now they were both laughing. Elizabeth wiped tears from the corners of her eyes, and Darcy allowed himself the kind of hearty guffaw he never usually indulged. It was some time before Elizabeth was calm enough to speak. "I never suspected. You are very sly, Mr. Darcy."

"I suppose." Darcy shrugged uncomfortably. "My actions occasioned me great uneasiness. I abhor deceit.

Such tactics should have been beneath me, but I was desperate. I could only think of annual visits to Rosings and seeing you married to that—" Darcy stopped himself before uttering words not fit for the presence of a lady.

"You could have simply declared your feelings."

"To another man's fiancée? It would not be honorable, and I was not certain you would accept."

She pursed her lips. "Hmm, perhaps not."

"I am proud and difficult, after all." He gave her a somewhat twisted smile. "It is rather lowering to think I might have be less preferable than Mr. Collins."

He had intended the statement as a joke, but Elizabeth seemed to take it seriously. She reached out for his hand, and Darcy thrilled at her touch—the first time she had initiated contact. "You improve greatly upon further acquaintance. Mr. Collins most definitely does not."

The pressure of her fingers on his hand warmed him from the inside out. He longed to kiss her again but feared he would fail to rein in his inappropriate desires.

Elizabeth intertwined their fingers. "I thank you for your honesty. You did not need to tell me. I never would have guessed."

"Do you forgive my interference?" That familiar pang of guilt pierced his heart. "Lord knows I never wished to cause you grief."

"Yes, of course," she said quickly. "All is forgiven and forgotten." A weight Darcy did not realize he was carrying was lifted off his shoulders. "It caused me momentary distress," Elizabeth continued, "but ultimately, it was best that I not marry Mr. Collins."

And marry me instead. But Elizabeth said nothing of the kind.

Darcy swallowed his disappointment; he had promised to give her time. "Indeed."

"Perhaps we should return to our beds. It would not do for your early-rising servants to find us here." Elizabeth smiled at him. Darcy hesitated, not sure whether he should voice the question in his mind. "I promise to consider your proposal today and believe I will be in a position to give you an answer by the end of the day."

How does she so unerringly guess what I think?

Darcy nodded, too full of feeling to speak. Elizabeth turned and strode toward the French doors leading to the gallery.

Once inside, Darcy closed the doors behind them and relit the candle, glancing at the room's tall clock. "I had not realized the late hour. It *is* past time I returned you to your bedchamber." He offered her his arm once more, and they strolled back to the stairs. Darcy was already regretting the necessity of letting her go. The unexpected encounter had been so pleasant.

She let out a breathy laugh. "I do not believe I am any sleepier than I was before. You did not help to lull me to sleep at all."

"A thousand pardons, madam." Darcy smiled, happy she was teasing him. "I do not believe I will sleep well either."

As they ascended the stairs, Elizabeth lifted her skirt to reveal a finely turned ankle and delicate feet inside her slippers. Darcy suppressed a moan but could not bring himself to avert his eyes. Was there any part of her that he did not find supremely attractive? He forced his attention back to her face where she regarded him with a raised eyebrow. He needed to say something to conceal his embarrassment. "The next time I kiss you, I will do my best to make it as dull as possible."

They had reached the top of the stairs. Elizabeth's expression was delightfully arch. "The next time, Mr. Darcy?"

He leaned in and whispered in her ear. "If I have my way, I will never stop kissing you."

When he pulled back, Elizabeth's eyes were closed. Hopefully, she was relishing the idea as much as he did— rather than suppressing her revulsion.

Opening her eyes, she straightened her shoulders and took a step back. Did she wish to escape him or simply maintain propriety? God forbid she would regard him as only a little better than Collins. She took a deep breath and opened her eyes. "I believe it is past time for me to retire." Her tone was firm.

"Of course," Darcy responded at once.

"Not that I am likely to *sleep* for some time." Her smile was mischievous. "At breakfast I will have dark circles under my eyes, and you will know that you are responsible."

Such sportive comments sent his thoughts racing in inappropriate directions. "I apologize beforehand." Darcy kissed her hand, wishing he dared to kiss her lips again. "Good night, Elizabeth."

"Good night." She turned and slipped away up the hall.

Before she had disappeared from sight, Darcy whispered, "Sweet dreams." But he did not know if she heard him.

***

Elizabeth was awake for hours after her return to her bedchamber and only dropped into a fitful slumber when the first light of dawn was creeping past her curtains.

It seemed she had only been asleep a few minutes, but it was full morning when she heard a commotion in the hallway. She had only groggily opened her eyes when Jane burst through her door without knocking. Elizabeth took one look at her stricken face and struggled into a sitting position. "What is the matter?" Had someone learned of her moonlit walk with Mr. Darcy?

But then their Aunt Gardiner, dressed for traveling, entered the room behind Jane. Elizabeth's heart jolted in alarm. Her aunt carefully closed the door behind them.

Words tumbled from Jane's lips. "I am sorry to wake you so early, but…oh, Lizzy! Aunt Gardiner arrived with the most dreadful news! It is about Lydia."

Elizabeth's body surged with energy. "Is she well?"

"She has left Longbourn in the middle of the night and thrown herself into the power of Mr. Wickham!" Now Elizabeth understood the reason behind the pallor of her sister's skin.

Elizabeth covered her mouth, stifling a horrified gasp.

"She left a note for Papa saying they were going to Gretna Green, but Colonel Forster has traced them as far as London and says they are definitely not married!" Jane collapsed into a loveseat near the window. Aunt Gardiner sat next to her niece, taking her hand in comfort.

"Such an ill-advised match!" Elizabeth cried, tears streaming down her face. "He cannot possible love Lydia or care about her!"

Aunt Gardiner spoke. "Your father has arrived in London to seek them, and he would like you to return to Longbourn to help your mother. Your uncle and I were nearby at Lambton visiting some of my childhood friends. An express arrived during the night with the news. Since Pemberley is so close, we brought the carriage to convey you to London." Her brow was furrowed, but she maintained her composure better than Jane.

"Of course! We must leave at once." Elizabeth slid out of bed and shrugged on the dressing gown that had been lying on the coverlet.

Aunt Gardiner nodded briskly. "I will ask the maid to start packing Jane's trunk, and then she may start on yours." She looked at Elizabeth. "As it is still very early, perhaps you should pen a note to Mr. Darcy begging his forgiveness for leaving so precipitously. "

Elizabeth gasped as she recalled the previous night's events. "Mr. Darcy!" Her aunt's eyes widened. "He asked me—" Elizabeth shook her head with a sharp jerk, realizing she must keep the story to herself. "No, never mind."

The exchange had caught Jane's attention. "At the supper table last night, Mr. Darcy said—"

Elizabeth cut her sister off. "It hardly matters now, Jane." Mr. Darcy might have fancied himself in love with her the night before, but he would never wish to tie himself to a family mired in scandal—particularly involving Mr. Wickham! Her family's lack of status and wont of propriety meant she was a barely acceptable choice for him before, but now...

Even if by some miracle he still wanted her, she could not, in good conscience, accept his proposal. The thought caused an unaccustomed heaviness to settle in her chest. Last night, she had realized that all of his kindness and consideration toward her was not some sort of bizarre aberration but actually represented Mr. Darcy revealing his true heart to her. Indeed, she had been so touched by his sentiments that she had nearly accepted his proposal there, under the full moon. Only the shock and novelty of the situation had demanded she proceed with caution. She was now grateful she had held her peace, but the full realization of what she was losing gripped her, and her tears flowed even faster.

Her chances of happiness with Mr. Darcy were slipping away like water through her fingers. *It is for the best*, she told herself. *Once he hears of this scandal, he will want nothing to do with you or your family.* Better that he would not regret that he married her.

It was imperative that they depart before he arose. "Perhaps we should summon another maid," she suggested.

"We should leave as soon as possible." It would be hard enough to leave the beauty of Pemberley behind; a formal leave-taking from Mr. Darcy would make their departure nearly impossible for Elizabeth. No point in twisting the knife once it was in the wound.

"Maybe we should wait until Mr. Darcy is awake to tell him our goodbyes?" Aunt Gardiner suggested.

"I will write him a note," Elizabeth said hastily. "We should conceal these unhappy circumstances as long as possible, and it will be easier in writing."

"Very well." Her expression was dubious, but Elizabeth gave an inward sigh of relief. At least her aunt did not suspect the depths of her niece's cowardice.

"I will summon an extra maid. Your uncle is waiting downstairs, and the coach is outside. We could be on the road to London within the hour." Aunt Gardner was already striding to the door as she spoke. Elizabeth trudged toward the sitting room's desk, dreading the letter she must write.

Chapter 10

"Mr. Darcy?"

Darcy rolled over and groaned, aware that his valet had been calling his name for some time. He glanced at the clock on the mantle. Good Lord, he had had only been asleep for two hours! It had better be important. Rubbing his eyes, he stared blearily at the man. "What is it, Greeves?"

Greeves's brow was furrowed, his eyes wide as he held out a letter. "Miss Elizabeth Bennet asked Mr. Carter to deliver this letter to you."

Darcy hastily sat up, trying to wipe the cobwebs of sleep from his mind. Why would Elizabeth write a note rather than speak with him? Had she already decided to decline his proposal? A weight settled on his chest, constricting his breathing.

Darcy took the simple piece of paper but just held it as if it were a wild animal that might bite at any minute.

"The Miss Bennets are making ready to depart within the hour," Greeves said.

"What?" Darcy's head jerked up to stare at his valet, but the man shrugged. Was Elizabeth so desperate to escape him? Blast! She had seemed to welcome his advances on the terrace…but no, she must have tolerated him…he had rushed her. This was entirely his fault!

"The ladies' aunt and uncle arrived half an hour ago in a state of great agitation and needed to see the young ladies at once," Greeves said.

"Oh." Darcy rubbed a hand over his face, wishing for a greater state of alertness. That was a different matter. If relatives had arrived suddenly and unexpectedly, Elizabeth's departure was not likely to be a reaction to Darcy's behavior; however, he was now alarmed at the nature of the emergency that had called the women away.

"They commenced packing immediately. Miss Elizabeth asked Mr. Carter to give you the note after her departure, but we thought it best if you saw it at once."

Darcy's servants were worth every penny he paid them. "Good man." Darcy unfolded the letter with trembling hands.

> *Mr. Darcy,*
> *My Aunt and Uncle Gardiner arrived at the house this morning with news of an alarming nature regarding my youngest sister's whereabouts. We are leaving immediately for London to assist my family in their hour of need. The truth cannot be concealed long. In light of today's revelations, it is best if relations between our families are completely severed. You should not suffer for my family's mistakes. I am sorry circumstances did not prove otherwise.*
> *Yours always,*
> *E. B.*

Darcy opened his mouth, but no words emerged. He swallowed and tried again. "I will dress immediately."

"Very good, sir." Greeves gave his master a troubled look and left for the dressing room.

Darcy frantically scrutinized the letter again, reading between the lines; he must understand what Elizabeth had *not* said. Which sister was the youngest? He believed it was Lydia, the silliest, most flirtatious one. The chit must have eloped—or perhaps not got as far as Gretna Green; otherwise the family would not be seeking her in London. Silently, Darcy cursed the thoughtless girl. Elizabeth hardly needed another cause of anxiety.

By why did she wish to sever ties between their families? An elopement was not that great a scandal! Perhaps she was angry at the liberties he had taken the night before and was using her sister's elopement as an excuse? She should turn to him in her hour of need! Yet her impulse was to run from him and shun his company. The thought tasted bitter in his mouth.

Darcy crumpled the letter, falling back against his pillow. If she thought so little of him, perhaps he should simply let her go. A clean break.

But there was her adieu. What did she mean by "yours always?" To Darcy, that implied she would have chosen otherwise if she could.

Darcy threw off the covers and jumped out of bed. No, he would not let her go without a fight. Even if he had to follow her all the way to London!

***

As Elizabeth tied her bonnet ribbons, she thanked providence that they would escape from Pemberley without difficulty. Not that Mr. Darcy was likely to create trouble deliberately, but seeing him would make their departure infinitely harder.

Their trunks had been loaded onto the Gardiners' carriage, and the coachman was waiting. Her Uncle Gardiner had been awaiting the sisters near the front door and had exchanged grim hugs with Elizabeth when she had descended the stairs. Now he paced restlessly as they awaited Jane. Mr. Carter, Pemberley's butler, was watching Elizabeth anxiously and wringing his hands as if he wished to arrest their departure—or at least feed them a hearty breakfast first.

Finally, Jane descended the stairs and handed Mr. Carter a note for Miss Bingley. Intent on observing all the proprieties, Jane would not write to Mr. Bingley directly. Hopefully, his sister could be trusted to accurately report the contents of the letter. He could not be left with the impression that Jane had departed because of waning affections!

If they had only remained another day or so, Elizabeth was certain Mr. Bingley would have proposed. But the point was moot anyway. He might have withdrawn the offer once Lydia's disgrace became known. Her youngest sister's carelessness would damage the fortunes of the whole family. Elizabeth bit her lip as tears threatened to spill; there would be time enough for tears during the trip to London.

Elizabeth studied the front hallway intently, wishing to impress upon her memory the images of black and white marble tiles, the finely carved marble staircase, and many beautiful paintings on the walls. She would never visit again, but if she fixed it in her mind, she could return here in her thoughts.

Her vision went blurry. It would not do. She must not think about what else from Pemberley she would dearly miss.

Having finished her quiet conversation with Mr. Carter, Jane drifted over to Elizabeth, appearing as grim and miserable as Elizabeth felt. In ten or fifteen years, would they look back on this visit to Pemberley as a shining pinnacle of their youth? A moment when happiness seemed in their grasp? Tears stung the corners of her eyes, and Elizabeth blinked them back.

"Lizzy, it is past time," her uncle said. "The trip to London is a long one. We must leave immediately."

Elizabeth nodded. As the butler opened the grand, carved oak front doors, Elizabeth stored each detail in her memory. Jane took her arm, and they walked toward the carriage.

A tattoo of footsteps sounded on the marble staircase behind them, but she ignored it. However, the rapid tap-tap of boot heels announced that the latecomer was striding toward them.

"Eliz-Miss Bennet!" Mr. Darcy's voice was louder than necessary and echoed in the high-ceilinged room. "A word, please!"

Elizabeth closed her eyes, her chin sinking. They had come so close! She had almost escaped without facing this unpleasantness. Her chest constricted as she turned slowly to face him, releasing Jane's arm. She did owe him an explanation, no matter what it cost her.

"Mr. Darcy." She gave a small curtsey. "I regret that a family crisis necessitates our immediate departure."

Clearly, he had hastened to see them before they left. His hair lacked its usual careful grooming, he had not shaved, and he was still tugging his waistcoat into place. But these signs of dishevelment only added a roguish charm to his innately handsome appearance. *If I must leave him, why could he not at least look like an ogre?*

"Yes, I read your letter." His voice was not raised but held more than a hint of tension.

"You did?" Elizabeth shot a look at Mr. Carter, who was busily examining a piece of immaculately clean wainscoting. "I apologize, I did not wish you awakened at such an early hour."

Mr. Darcy waved away this objection. "Will you please tell me what I can do to be of assistance to your family?" He took her gloved hand in both of his.

Her uncle frowned and took a few steps forward.

Elizabeth's heart melted even as she shook her head. Mr. Darcy would not be so eager to volunteer if he knew the identity of Lydia's seducer. "You have already done so much for us."

Her Aunt Gardiner was regarding Elizabeth speculatively as if she believed Mr. Darcy *could* be of assistance, but she did not know of Georgiana's previous experience with Wickham. Elizabeth could not ask Mr. Darcy to allow the man back into his life. She gave her aunt a quelling look accompanied by a slight shake of the head.

Mr. Darcy was watching her intently. Had he noticed their silent conversation?

"We thank you for your hospitality; we are sorry to cut our visit short." Regarding him steadily, she tried to imbue her words with additional layers of meaning. She would never see him again, but at least if she conveyed some of her regret, it might help ease his heartache. Nothing would help hers. "If I had my choice, I would never leave Pemberley."

Mr. Darcy's eyes lit up. "Indeed?"

"But, of course, that is impossible," Elizabeth added hastily. If they lingered any longer, she would soon abandon her resolve to leave. It was all too clear what she must do. She turned toward the door.

"Miss Bennet." Mr. Darcy's voice had a new hint of steel.

Reluctantly she turned back. "Mr. Darcy?"

His mouth was set in a grim line. "I will not release you from our engagement."

Her aunt's mouth dropped open in amazement, and her uncle took another step closer to them, his frown deepening.

It took Elizabeth a moment to understand what Mr. Darcy meant. She forced out a laugh. "There is no engagement!" She turned her gaze on her aunt and uncle. "'Tis only a joke—something he said to shock Miss Bingley."

"I *will not* let you go." He regarded her with a burning ferocity.

Would he force her to marry him? Would she be in the unbelievable position of marrying one of the most sought-after men in England *against her will*?

"Mr. Darcy, you do not understand the nature of Lydia's—" Elizabeth began.

"I do not care about your family's actions, Elizabeth. I only care about your feelings for me." His tone of voice, his eyes, every line of his body was begging her to reconsider.

I should simply tell him I do not care for him in that way. It would be the easiest route. She opened her mouth to say so, but then closed it again. She could never convince him of her indifference. Undoubtedly, her face betrayed her feelings even now.

No, she must speak plainly. "There will be scandal attached to my family. I do not wish to have your good name associated with it."

The muscles in Mr. Darcy's jaw twitched. "I do not care about scandal or my family's name. I only care about your response regarding the matter we discussed last night on the terrace…after we kissed."

Jane gasped. Her Aunt Gardiner covered her mouth, her eyes wide. Her uncle's face turned red.

Elizabeth closed her eyes and lowered her head; her cheeks must be scarlet. Mr. Darcy had just admitted in front of her aunt and uncle and sister—and his servants— that they had been alone together at night. That he had *kissed* her. Her uncle would never overlook such a breach of propriety.

Damn the man!

Uncle Gardiner took a step closer to Mr. Darcy, somehow managing to look intimidating despite being foot shorter than the younger man. "Are you admitting that you had my niece alone with you in this house last night, and you *kissed* her?"

"Yes." Darcy's answer was calm. "More than once."

"Lizzy?" Her uncle's eyes remained on Mr. Darcy, but the anger in his voice was directed at her.

She swallowed hard. "I had a nightmare…"

"And?" His voice held no hint of patience.

"I took a stroll about Pemberley to help me sleep after the nightmare," Elizabeth clarified.

Uncle Gardiner rolled his eyes. "Did he or did he not kiss you?"

"Yes." Even to her own ears Elizabeth's voice sounded small. "But nothing more than a few kisses."

There was a slight sound from the top of the stairs where Miss and Mr. Bingley apparently had been standing for some time. Miss Bingley's face was aghast while Mr. Bingley seemed bemused.

Elizabeth longed to bury her face in her hands. Now her humiliation was complete.

Her uncle's voice shook with anger. "I do not pretend to understand everything that has passed between you, but I know one thing: if you have kissed her, sir, you have compromised her reputation and must be prepared to do the right thing."

"I understand, sir." Mr. Darcy's expression was solemn but not ashamed. However, when he turned his gaze to Elizabeth, he quirked a smile at one corner of his mouth.

Elizabeth pursed her lips, attempting to keep furious words from exploding out of her mouth. He had made a betrothal necessary, but he did not know he was tying himself to a family haunted by a scandal involving Wickham!

If only she had been less circumspect in her note. If she had explained the nature of the problem, he would have understood why they could not marry. Even if she had confessed it moments ago…but now it was too late. When he learned the truth, he would be furious; he would feel trapped.

Mr. Darcy's next words were more conciliatory in tone; perhaps he finally noticed the fury emanating from her pores. "I understand how eager you are to depart for London. However, since I am your *fiancé*, we should discuss the situation and arrive at a plan." He waved in the general direction of his study. Elizabeth nodded her head stiffly.

"Very well, I will join you in five minutes." At these words from her uncle, Mr. Darcy looked startled. He had not counted on Mr. Gardiner's supervision, but Elizabeth knew her uncle's strict sense of propriety.

"Perhaps we may retire to my study?" Mr. Darcy suggested.

Elizabeth nodded again but said nothing, afraid of what might fly from her mouth if she opened it. She merely followed Mr. Darcy as he led the way past the stairs and down the hallway. It felt strange to be visiting his private space without the need for a chaperone.

Mr. Darcy closed the door softly behind her as they entered the study. "I apologize, Elizabeth." His voice was low and rough.

"For what?" Keeping her eyes fixed on the fireplace at the other end of the room, she refused to turn around and look at him. "For compromising my reputation, or for telling everyone that you had?"

Mr. Darcy sighed and walked to his desk. "I will not apologize for kissing you unless you wish me to. It was a true expression of my sentiments." He rubbed his chin. "But perhaps I should not have blurted it out in such a fashion."

"Oh, do you think so?" Elizabeth's tone was sharp enough to cut rope. "You said you would grant me time to make a decision, and now you have taken matters into your own hands." Crossing her arms, she fixed her eyes on the carpet.

"I did," Mr. Darcy blew out a breath, "but the note you gave Carter made it clear you had already decided."

"As was my prerogative!" she spat. "You did not tell me you had no intention of honoring my decision."

He stared at the floor and, for a long moment, said nothing. "You are correct." He swallowed. "And I apologize." He raised his head and looked her in the eye. "Your note suggested you were refusing to marry me because of your sister's scandal and its effect on my reputation. I did not find that to be sufficient cause."

This stirred Elizabeth's ire again. "Why should *you* decide what is a good reason? Is it not my choice?"

"Yes, but—" Mr. Darcy sank into the chair behind the desk, his back bowed and his shoulders hunched. "I confess…When I read the note I…panicked." His voice was hoarse, almost a whisper. "I was terrified of losing you. I feared if you walked through that door, I would never see you again."

I thought so as well.

He tugged at his cravat as if it were choking him. "I could not bear the thought of losing you, particularly over something as trivial as my reputation."

Abruptly, Elizabeth's anger melted and ran out of her body. Now she realized she had caused him so much pain. She had assumed he would be better off without her and her family's scandal, but perhaps she was not the best judge.

When she said nothing, Mr. Darcy continued on, collapsing further into his chair. "I did not consider the possibility that you were using your sister's elopement as a way to ease the sting of rejecting my offer." He was not looking at her, rubbing his eyes with the heels of his hands. "If you do not believe you can return my sentiments—"

"No!" Elizabeth took two quick steps toward him until she was beside his chair. "I do return—I mean, I do think I can—that was not my purpose in writing the note." Boldly, she reached over and pulled his hands from his eyes. "My concern for your family's reputation was my only reservation. My feelings for you…were not reflected in that note."

Mr. Darcy stood quickly but then leaned against the edge of the desk as if he needed the support. Was he truly so relieved?

However, he does not know the whole story, she reminded herself. "You do not comprehend the entirety of the problem," she told him.

He regarded her warily.

"As you surmised, Lydia has run off—with Mr. Wickham."

Breath hissed through his teeth, and he sank again into the chair, staring at the ceiling. This was the reaction she feared. Elizabeth turned her gaze to the fireplace. "I knew you would not wish to marry into a family connected with Mr. Wickham," she continued. "I thought we should leave before the scandal became widely known."

A muscle worked in his jaw as he ground his teeth, but Darcy leaned forward and took both of her hands in his, quickly stripping off her gloves so he could touch bare skin. "I do find this news distressing, in part because I feel it is my fault. I should have made Wickham's character more generally known in Meryton. Then he would not have been able to impose himself on your sister this way!"

"No!" she exclaimed. "You take too much upon yourself."

He shook his head, gazing down at their clasped hands. "In any case, I have no reservations about marrying you—for this or any other reason."

Despite her own reservations, Elizabeth felt something inside loosen at this declaration. "But Wickham could become my brother-in-law!"

"That might occasion some unpleasantness, but it would be nothing compared to the pain of losing you." She could hear the strain in his voice. "I love you so very much."

Something inside Elizabeth thrilled at the sound of those words. She had guessed his feelings, but he had not actually declared them before. Suddenly, *her* feelings for him came sharply into focus. *How did I not see it before?* Tears fell for a second time that day but for a completely different reason. "And I love you."

His eyes were alive with hope. "You will be my wife?"

"I will."

Had such a broad smile ever before graced Mr. Darcy's face? He was always so serious, but suddenly, he seemed almost giddy. He tugged her hands until she was seated on his lap, and he immediately enveloped her in his arms. The kiss he bestowed on her had none of the tentativeness of the previous night. This kiss expressed his joy and wonderment that she was to be his. He plunged his fingers into her hair, heedless of the hairpins cascading to the floor, and cradled her head in his hands. His lips were warm, and his tongue was insistent in demanding entrance to her mouth. It was a sensual duet she wished would never end.

The door creaked open. "Darcy, I—" The voice was Mr. Bingley's.

Elizabeth sprang off Mr. Darcy's lap, but Mr. Bingley was already in the room, his eyes wide and his cheeks reddening.

"P-perhaps I should g-go," he stammered.

"No, stay. We must discuss travel plans. I will be leaving, as will the Miss Bennets." Mr. Darcy spoke to Bingley, but his eyes were watching Elizabeth with a barely banked fire. His gaze held her mesmerized; she knew she must present a sight, with her hair half down and her clothing disheveled.

"V-very well."

Elizabeth understood Mr. Bingley's hesitancy; Mr. Darcy hardly looked like a man ready to discuss travel plans. He glanced at the clock on the mantle and addressed Elizabeth. "Your uncle will be here in a minute."

"Oh!" Elizabeth hurriedly bent to collect the hair pins that had fallen to the carpet.

"I would like to accompany you and the Gardiners to London, if you do not mind delaying your departure by an hour or so. I believe I can be of assistance in locating Wickham."

"Wickham!" Mr. Bingley exclaimed.

Darcy finally turned his gaze to his friend. "Indeed. I will explain."

Having collected all the pins, Elizabeth hastened from the room. Hopefully, their betrothal would excuse their improprieties in her uncle's eyes, but she needed to fix her hair before anyone else saw her!

Chapter 11

Mr. Bennet was not happy. He hugged his daughters with a grim smile, but his jaw was set, and he appeared close to the end of his endurance. His face was gray, and his posture was far more stooped than Darcy recalled. It made him more determined than ever to relieve the older man of the burden Wickham's actions had created.

Nevertheless, Elizabeth's father shook Darcy's hand with an ironic twinkle in his eye. "Mr. Darcy, I am pleased you saw fit to finally return my daughters to me." As jokes went, it was rather a barbed one, but Darcy was careful to take no notice. His future father-in-law was not likely to be pleased about the manner of their betrothal.

Their coach had arrived at Gracechurch Street just as Mr. Bennet had returned from a fruitless day of searching for Lydia and Wickham. Mrs. Gardiner had left immediately to check on her children, but the rest of the party had followed Mr. Bennet's shuffling gait into the home's rather small parlor where the two older men had discussed all that had been done to locate the wayward pair. However, when Darcy suggested he could assist in the search, Mr. Bennet was not amenable.

"I thank you for your offer, but we have quite enough cooks in this particular soup as it is." Mr. Bennet flicked a piece of dust from the sleeve of his coat.

"Papa, Mr. Darcy has particular knowledge of Mr. Wickham. They grew up together," Elizabeth offered.

"Indeed?" Mr. Bennet peered at Darcy through his spectacles. "Then pray you, young man, can you tell me why you did not warn my family about this rascal? I come to find out he has meddled with the daughters of tradesmen in Meryton and run up debts all over the town!"

This was not an auspicious beginning, but only the truth would do. "Believe me, sir, I have been castigating myself for this oversight for days. I did not wish to lay bare my family's private dealings, and other families have suffered as a result." He refused to look away from Mr. Bennet's face. "I wish to atone for my oversight by helping you locate your daughter."

"Hmph." Mr. Bennet turned his gaze to the fireplace.

Mr. Gardiner looked at his brother and then at Darcy. "Naturally, we do not hold you responsible—" Mr. Bennet made an inarticulate grunt but said nothing, and his brother-in-law continued, ignoring the interruption. "But thank you, nonetheless, for you kind offer." The man raised his voice and looked meaningfully at Elizabeth's father. "It seems we are sorely in need of assistance."

Mr. Bennet crossed his arms over his chest and said nothing, which was a sort of victory in itself. Elizabeth then knelt by her father's chair, placing her hand on his arm. "Papa, please let Mr. Darcy help. You look so tired. You should rest."

Mr. Bennet's expression softened as he gazed on his second daughter. "My dearest Lizzy. It is good to have you back with us, but I am afraid things will go ill with you in Meryton." His voice lowered to a growl. "The day before Lydia ran away, I received a letter from Mr. Collins. That idiot parson has treated you very ill! Why did you not see fit to inform us?"

"Do not trouble yourself about that." She patted her father's arm again. "All will be well."

"All will be well? Mr. Collins has also been corresponding with Sir William Lucas! Lady Lucas has told half of Meryton! Do you know what horrible rumors are floating about the countryside?" The man's face was turning an alarming shade of red. Such agitation could not be good for his constitution.

Elizabeth shot a look at Darcy, and he nodded slightly. He had thought to delay discussion of the engagement until Mr. Bennet was in better spirits, but doing so now might help ease his mind.

Elizabeth stood. "Jane, perhaps we should see how our cousins have grown?"

"Yes, of course!" Jane stood hastily, and the two women hurried out of the room, leaving Darcy with the two older gentlemen. Mr. Gardiner scowled at him, perhaps recalling how the master of Pemberley had conducted his betrothal to date.

He took a deep breath and drew himself up straight. This would not be an easy conversation. Before he could speak, Mr. Bennet stood and shuffled to the sideboard where he poured a generous quantity of brandy and then seated himself again.

"Mr. Bennet, I had another matter to discuss with you."

"Oh?" The other man stared at his brandy.

"I have asked for Miss Elizabeth's hand in marriage, and she has consented."

Bennet's hand jerked and brandy sloshed over the rim of his glass. With an oath, he set it down on the table near his chair and ignored the stain on his waistcoat. "What did you say?"

"Elizabeth and I are engaged."

Mr. Bennet's expression hardened. "Not if I say you are not."

"She is nearly of age to give her own consent," Darcy pointed out, then immediately chastised himself. He did not wish to start this conversation with an argument. "I love your daughter very much."

"You do?" Mr. Bennet's voice dripped acid. "I thought you found her not pretty enough to tempt you."

Darcy clenched his teeth. Were those careless words to haunt him for the rest of his life?

The other man took a generous gulp of his brandy. "Everyone in Meryton knows you are a proud, unpleasant sort of man. Why should I wish my daughter to marry you?"

Darcy took a deep breath, trying to slow his breathing and calm his agitated nerves before responding. Why did he have to encounter the one man in England who would not be thrilled to have his daughter marry for ten thousand a year? For a fleeting moment, Darcy wished he were having this conversation with *Mrs. Bennet*, but all things considered, the lack of smelling salts was a blessing.

"I regret not giving a better impression in Hertfordshire," he told Mr. Bennet. "I am not always at my best in society, but I hope you will give me an opportunity to change your mind. I daresay Elizabeth's opinion of me has improved."

Mr. Bennet regarded him with narrowed eyes. "Has it? Or is it simply her opinion of your ten thousand a year?"

Darcy clenched his fists, resisting the urge to stand. "Sir, you may say what you wish about me, but do not cast aspersions on your daughter's character!"

Mr. Gardiner shifted in his chair, drawing Darcy's gaze. He was nodding in approval of that response.

Darcy expected Mr. Bennet to start shouting, but instead, he sat back in his chair with a slight smile quirking up one corner of his mouth. Had that been some sort of test? "What will you do if I do not give my consent?" Mr. Bennet asked.

"I will wait until Elizabeth is of age." Darcy strove to keep his voice steady.

The other man frowned. "You are so confident she would go against my wishes?"

Darcy rubbed his chin, knowing he needed to step carefully. "I am confident Elizabeth loves me." It was fortunate Mr. Gardiner had not yet spoken of how Darcy had compromised Elizabeth's reputation. Her father was quite angry enough with Darcy as it was.

Mr. Bennet's gaze held his for several long seconds;
Darcy was careful not to look away. Finally, the older man
took a sip of his brandy. "Very well, I will speak with
Elizabeth. If things are as you say, I will give my consent."

Darcy breathed a sigh of relief. "Thank you, sir. I
do apologize for the irregular circumstances."

Mr. Bennet waved this away with a bemused smile.
"I would hardly expect Elizabeth to go about such matters
in the conventional way."

Mr. Gardiner stood hastily, perhaps happy to have
the business concluded. "Mr. Darcy, would you care to
join us in a glass of brandy? We should discuss how you
believe we might locate Lydia and Wickham."

Darcy accepted a glass gladly and re-seated himself
opposite Mr. Bennet, who was rubbing his chest with a
rather pained expression.

"Are you not feeling well?" Darcy asked.

The other man muttered "chest pain" in the same
tone one might say "a trifling cold."

Darcy could not suppress his sense of alarm. "Have
you seen a doctor?"

"Aye, but he cannot do a damn thing! He suggested
a warm bath." Mr. Bennet snorted. "The pain *does* worsen
under stressful circumstances." He downed the last of his
brandy.

Darcy could only imagine the sort of stress Mr.
Bennet had experienced recently. Knowing his wife and
daughters were vulnerable after his death, he must have
been hoping for Jane's engagement to Bingley. Darcy felt
a sharp pang of guilt over his actions there. Then
Elizabeth's engagement to Collins seemed to secure their
future, only to have it unravel. Now Lydia's scandal
threatened to ruin the reputations of all the sisters.

He took a sip of brandy. If Mr. Bennet came to see
him as a worthy son-in-law, it might alleviate some of his
anxiety. However, the man's face was deeply lined and

graying; perhaps his concerns about Darcy's character were too great. Darcy hoped he could marry Elizabeth soon. If her father should pass on, he needed to be in a position to help the family immediately. Why had he not proposed earlier? They might be happily wed by now, and Darcy might have prevented the difficulties with Wickham.

"Perhaps you simply need the right doctor," Darcy suggested. "I have a physician here in London whom I highly recommend, if you would be willing to have him see you."

Mr. Bennet frowned at him for a minute. "Yes, yes, fine." He waved his hand wearily.

"Perhaps we may resolve this situation with Wickham quickly, and you may return home," Darcy said.

Mr. Bennet shifted uncomfortably in his chair. "We can hope." His tone suggested he thought this as likely as an ice storm in hell.

Darcy met Mr. Gardiner's eyes across the room, and they shared a moment of silent concern. Darcy cleared his throat. "Very well, let me tell you what I know of Wickham's haunts and acquaintances…"

***

The following afternoon, a strange delegation packed into the Gardiners' carriage and made its way to one of the more disreputable parts of London. Mr. Bennet had been insistent on joining the expedition, but a severe attack of chest pain necessitated that he take to his bed. Despite his concerns for the other man's health, Darcy thought it might be easier dealing with Wickham on his own.

However, he had been unable to dissuade Elizabeth from accompanying them. Darcy loathed the idea of exposing her to the town's seamy underbelly, but Elizabeth had made the irrefutable argument that her sister was living in that underbelly and might be in need of assistance. Darcy had finally relented but had brought along the Gardiners' maid, Mary, and his own footman, Hawkins, for her comfort and protection. As he regarded the grim faces in the carriage, Darcy wished he could have visited Wickham alone.

The carriage lurched to a stop, and Mr. Gardiner disembarked, followed by Darcy. He glanced around at the houses crowded together, the grimy cobblestones, and ragged street urchins watching them with gleaming eyes. He turned and fixed Elizabeth with a glare. "You *will* remain in the carriage." This had been part of their agreement. She should be safe enough in the carriage with another woman—and the coachman and footman.

"Yes, of course, William." Her eyes were wide and earnest, but somehow, he had no faith that she would actually follow through on her promise given the right provocation. But there was nothing for it.

Fighting off a chill of apprehension, he closed and securely latched the door. "Hawkins!" he called.

The footman hurried around from the other side of the vehicle. "Sir?"

"Do not allow Miss Bennet to leave the carriage for any reason."

"Y-yes, sir." Hawkins's expression was dubious, and Darcy could understand why. He had no idea how the footman would stop Elizabeth if she took it into her head to venture out. Darcy could not imagine Hawkins laying hands on a lady.

As he and Mr. Gardiner strode across the street, Darcy reassured himself that he was worrying over nothing. Wickham and Lydia might be gone. Mrs. Younge could only say where they had been lodging two days ago. Even if they were at the pub, nothing might come of the visit, although he was determined to return Lydia to Gracechurch Street.

In the pub's downstairs room, Darcy paused to speak briefly to the man behind the bar. At least *he* believed Wickham was still renting the room upstairs. That much was promising. Darcy's face was grim as he climbed the narrow stairs, Mr. Gardiner's boots tapping behind him.

He hoped, for Mr. Bennet's sake, that Wickham was within and that they would resolve the matter hastily. Elizabeth's father did not look good; in fact, he seemed on the verge of apoplexy. If they were unable to reach a satisfactory accommodation with Wickham, it would only cause more strain on Mr. Bennet's weakened heart.

Darcy rapped on the door of the room at the top of the stairs. When there was no response, he rapped again, more loudly. Finally, the door opened a foot to reveal Wickham's unshaven face. He tried to close the door, but Darcy's boot prevented it.

Next to Darcy, Mr. Gardiner pushed the door wider. Over Wickham's shoulder, he could see Lydia sitting up in the room's bed, her hair disheveled, wearing nothing but a chemise. She giggled when she saw the men and pulled up a sheet to cover her chest. "Oh, Lord! Mr. Darcy! And Uncle Gardiner! Fancy seeing you here!"

Mr. Gardiner gave Wickham a hard shove in the chest, and the man staggered backward into the room. When he had regained his balance, Wickham essayed a ghost of his usual jaunty smile. "Darcy, my friend, what a pleasure to see you." He turned to the other man. "And you must be Lydia's uncle, whom she has mentioned so often."

Darcy hated to see that charm turned to such purposes. "Wickham," he growled. "We are here to return to Miss Lydia to her family."

"I shan't go!" Lydia cried.

Ignoring her, Darcy continued. "And to ensure that you do your duty and marry her."

Wickham nodded vigorously. "Yes, of course, you are right, Darcy. I must marry her."

Darcy narrowed his eyes as he regarded the contrite-looking man in front of him. Such immediate capitulation was completely uncharacteristic. What was Wickham's angle?

Mr. Gardiner turned to Lydia. "Lydia, dear, you must put on some clothes. We will take you to our house on Gracechurch Street."

"No! I shan't go! I like it here with my Wickham!" If Miss Lydia had been standing up, she undoubtedly would have stamped her foot. "You don't want me to go, do you?" She addressed the last high-pitched question to Wickham, but he was no longer there. He had taken advantage of the momentary distraction to bolt out of the open door.

With an oath, Darcy raced down the narrow stairs, but Wickham had quite a head start. He had barely reached the bottom of the stairs when he saw Wickham hurrying out the pub's door and into the afternoon sunshine.

"Stop that man! Wickham!" Darcy cried, but the pub's inhabitants only glanced around with mild curiosity.

Damnation! Once Wickham was on the streets of London, he could disappear anywhere, and it could take weeks to find him again.

Darcy ran through the busy pub but could not avoid colliding with a barmaid. They both collapsed in a tangle of limbs. Darcy picked himself up and spared a moment to make sure the young woman was unharmed, averting his eyes from her copious bosom. Finally, he made it through the door, knowing it was futile. He would never find Wickham now.

Darcy could scarcely believe the sight that met his eyes. Wickham was sprawled face first on the cobblestones a few yards from the entrance to the inn. He was screaming and thrashing about but was completely unable to stand—because Elizabeth and the Gardiners' maid were sitting on him.

Elizabeth was demurely perched on his back while the maid was sitting on his legs. A few feet away, Hawkins was picking himself up off the cobblestones; an angry red mark on his cheek suggested that Wickham had hit him.

Wickham spotted Darcy as he exited the pub. "Darcy! Get these crazy women off me!" Darcy could not help laughing at the absurd sight. "Darcy! They are lunatics!" Wickham cried.

Darcy gestured to his footman. "Hawkins, we need a bit of rope."

The footman was back in a moment. After Elizabeth and the maid stood and dusted themselves off, Hawkins and Darcy bound Wickham's hands behind his back.

Wickham grumbled about kidnapping and imprisonment, but Darcy reminded him about his creditors, who would surely demand debtors' gaol. After that, Wickham subsided into a sullen silence.

Hawkins hustled Wickham into the carriage while Darcy carefully inspected Elizabeth. She laughed. "I am unharmed, William!"

"How did this come to pass?" he asked, holding her firmly by the shoulders.

"It occurred to me that Wickham might try to run from his responsibilities, so I asked Hawkins to guard the door. When I heard you yelling Wickham's name, I left the carriage." She gave him an apologetic smile. "Wickham struck poor Hawkins in the face, but he was not looking where he was going. I tripped him, and then Mary and I sat on him so he could not escape."

Darcy laughed, impressed by his fiancée's ingenuity. "Very well, perhaps I will forgive you for leaving the carriage."

***

As Elizabeth had noticed before, events proceeded quite rapidly when Mr. Darcy set his mind to it. A virtual prisoner at Darcy House, Wickham complained vociferously about Lydia and her annoying, vexing ways. He denied any desire to marry her, but finally, he capitulated—after a sum was agreed upon and a posting was secured in a Northern regiment.

Lydia had been removed to Gracechurch Street where she proclaimed loudly that she missed "her Wickham" and did not see what all the fuss was about. Elizabeth was grateful that the Gardiners lived near a park where she could take very long walks.

Within three days, Mr. Darcy had obtained a special license, and Lydia and Wickham were wed. Elizabeth thought she had never attended a wedding where so many faces were so singularly grim. The noticeable exception was Lydia, who seemed delighted despite the circumstances. The "happy" couple was immediately dispatched to the North, although they were to have a stay of precisely one night at Longbourn before they left. Elizabeth was not sorry to miss their visit.

Mr. Bingley and his sisters had arrived in London a day behind Mr. Darcy and his party. He had been a regular visitor to Gracechurch Street where his buoyant good spirits had been a balm to her father as well as Jane. The day after the business with Lydia and Wickham was concluded, Mr. Bingley called on Jane and asked for her hand. Her father happily granted his consent; his only reservation was how many paroxysms of joy the news would occasion in his wife.

Elizabeth had happily observed how her father's health had improved steadily since the business with Wickham had been resolved. His color had improved, and he seemed to have greater energy and appetite. As she had suspected, his improved acquaintance with Mr. Darcy only enhanced his admiration for her fiancé, and she knew they were on the path to becoming friends.

Mr. Darcy's doctor called on her father the day after their fateful visit to Wickham's lodgings. Of all the occurrences during that visit to London, this event occasioned Elizabeth the most joy. He pronounced her father's heart problems to be not nearly as severe as the doctor in Hertfordshire had warned. He suggested that Mr. Bennett eat less to lose some weight, in addition to spending less time inside with his books and more time outside in the fresh air getting some exercise. Her grateful father resolved on taking daily walks. Elizabeth planned on enlisting Kitty's help in this endeavor. Kitty enjoyed walking and would be happy to accompany their father after her older sisters were married and gone.

Elizabeth had spent a fortnight at the Gardiners and was eager to be at Longbourn. When she and Jane had traveled to Rosings Park, they had only expected to be gone for a week at most! Finally, it was decided they would depart for Hertfordshire. Mr. Darcy needed to remain in London for some matters of business but would proceed to Longbourn after a few days. Mr. Bingley would transport Mr. Bennet and his daughters to their home and then stay at Netherfield—which Elizabeth thought not quite far enough away from her mother, who did not yet know about either engagement. When Mrs. Bennet learned the news, no doubt her future son-in-law would be able to hear her exclamations of joy even from three miles' distance.

However, Elizabeth's homecoming did not proceed at all as she expected. When they alighted from the carriage, her mother hurried out to greet them warmly, with many professions of delight. Then she turned to her second eldest daughter and exclaimed, "Lizzy, I am very happy you are here! Mr. Collins arrived last night and is very desirous of seeing you!"

Chapter 12

Elizabeth exchanged bewildered glances with Jane. What could Mr. Collins possibly have to say to her? Her shoulders slumped; after a long journey, a conversation about the wainscoting at Rosings was not to her liking. But there was nothing for it.

"Very well, Mama. I will refresh myself and then talk to him directly."

"He will meet you in the drawing room! Perhaps he is here to apologize and beg you to take him back!" Mrs. Bennet whispered loudly in Elizabeth's ear.

Elizabeth rolled her eyes. It was more likely Lady Catherine had learned of Elizabeth's engagement to Mr. Darcy and expected Mr. Collins to dissuade her from it.

A short while later, Elizabeth reluctantly opened the door to the drawing room. If only Jane could have accompanied her! But her mother had insisted that Mr. Collins wished to speak with her alone. The thought made Elizabeth's stomach churn in revulsion, and she resolved to dispense with the unpleasantness quickly.

Mr. Collins was on the far side of the room when she closed the door, but the moment she entered, he rushed across the space separating them and flung himself at her feet.

"Mr. Collins!" Elizabeth cried in alarm.

"My dearest Elizabeth!" Mr. Collins spoke to her shoes. "Can you ever forgive me for my horrible, unjust, unforgivable treatment of you?"

Elizabeth's nerves were thoroughly discomposed by this unexpected act. "Yes, yes, I forgive you! Please stand up!"

Mr. Collins raised his eyes to her face, reminding her uncomfortably of a puppy begging for a treat. "I cannot arise until I have begged, most abjectly, for you to grant me a place in your heart once more."

Elizabeth might have encountered more awkward situations in her life before, but she would have been hard-pressed to think of one at that moment. Attempting to put some space between them, she took several steps backward until she bumped against the door. Undeterred, Mr. Collins shuffled forward on his knees until he was again crouched right at her feet.

She cast about for the right words. No etiquette books she had read had prepared her for this situation. "Er...yes...of course...we may be friends once more, Mr. Collins. You are my cousin..."

"Will you not call me by my Christian name once again, my dearest, lovely one?"

Elizabeth neglected to point out that she had not used his first name even when they were engaged. Surely he did not believe—

"Say you will take me back into your arms, my honeysuckle rose!" he cried. "Tell me all is not lost!" Elizabeth rather hoped that whoever did marry Mr. Collins would hide his collection of lurid novels.

"Surely you are not suggesting that we should be betrothed once again?" she exclaimed.

"Yes, of course! I should never have let you go. It was wrong and foolish of me." He grabbed one of her hands with both of his. They were warm and sweaty. "I now see that we are formed perfectly for each other. No one else would suit me as well. I know no one else would suit you at all."

An icy coldness washed over Elizabeth, and she yanked her hand from his grasp, stalking to the window. She was now confident of Lady Catherine's role in Mr. Collins's sudden reappearance at Longbourn. "No one else? Not even Mr. Darcy?"

She glanced over her shoulder to see his reaction. He did not attempt to dissemble, but his face hardened. "A marriage to Mr. Darcy cannot take place; it *will not* take place. His aunt will not allow it." He walked on his knees halfway across the drawing room floor but then gave up and stood, slowly and creakily.

"I do not believe she is in a position to prevent it," Elizabeth responded.

"No! It is impossible. He may have been taken in by your arts and allurements, but he will come to his senses before any ceremony takes place. Better to accept me. Then you will not quit the sphere to which you are accustomed." Now his face was twisted into a nasty smile. "Another offer might never come your way. You might end up alone for your entire life."

She knew Mr. Collins was manipulating her, yet Elizabeth could not prevent herself from envisioning such a bleak future yawning before her like a bottomless chasm. It was all too easy to imagine: no husband or children, no home to call her own. Perhaps forced to seek work…

But a little question niggled at the back of her brain. "If Lady Catherine is so certain her nephew will throw me over, why did she send you here to lure me away from him?" She fixed Mr. Collins with a sharp glare.

Mr. Collins's eyes darted around the room. "Er…she…um…well, she did not wish you to be alone and suffer the effects of his rejection."

"Despite my arts and allurements?"

"Such trickery only lasts a short time." Mr. Collins's eyes narrowed as he regarded her.

"Then I wonder why you would ally yourself with a woman who practices it."

The man stared blankly at her for a moment. "I…um…Christian forgiveness demands—"

Elizabeth crossed her arms over her chest, wishing she had some way to force Mr. Collins to leave. "If Lady Catherine has concerns about my suitability for her nephew, she should discuss them with Mr. Darcy."

"She did. She called on him today."

A tremor shook Elizabeth, and she grew even colder. Lady Catherine might right now be at Darcy House, convincing her beloved William that he should not love her, that she did not deserve him…

The dark, bottomless chasm reappeared before her. If he rejected her, she would have nothing. She would be the subject of gossip in Meryton for months. Maybe she should reconsider….

Then she took another look at Mr. Collins's simpering face, his greasy hair, his stooped posture. No. A life as a spinster would be far preferable. She could live at Netherfield with Jane and Mr. Bingley.

With that resolution in place, Elizabeth decided to put an end to this farce. "I believe you were correct the first time. We do not suit, and we could not make each other happy. I wish you good day."

She strode with determination toward the door, but as she passed Mr. Collins, he grabbed her by the shoulders and pulled her toward him. Before she could resist, he was kissing her, although "kiss" was not an accurate label; it could best be described as a mashing of her lips by his—which were thin and overly wet. Elizabeth struggled to get away from him, but he held her in an iron grip.

She was vaguely aware of muffled sounds and people speaking in the corridor outside. Without warning, the door swung open and someone entered. Oh, thank goodness!

Mr. Collins lifted his head to see who had entered the room. But the next second, a fist met his jaw, and he traveled backward at a great rate of speed, landing on the carpet under the window in an undignified heap. Elizabeth lifted her eyes to see a seething Darcy, dusty from travel, glaring at Mr. Collins as if daring him to stand up and risk another blow.

Mr. Collins wisely remained where he was.

Heavens! William had found her kissing another man! Would he be angry with her? Would he break the engagement? The yawning chasm now engulfed her. She was trembling from head to toe but could not make herself move; she could merely stare at him.

When it became clear that Mr. Collins would not fight, William's stance relaxed, and he turned to Elizabeth. She felt paralyzed by his gaze—a rabbit in a hunter's sights.

"My darling!" He took one step toward her and wrapped her in his arms. The sense of being completely embraced was infinitely comforting. "Did that toad hurt you?" He pulled her head to his chest, soothing her with the vibrations of his deep, rumbling voice.

"No," Elizabeth said. "But I did not wish to kiss him, William. I did not!"

She pulled away to view his face and was relieved to see his rather sweet smile. "I know, my dear." His hand brushed lightly over her hair. "I have no doubt on that score. You would rather kiss an actual toad." Mr. Collins made a noise of objection from the floor, but a glare from William silenced him.

William's fingertips gently brushed her cheek. "I had a visit from my aunt immediately after you left London, and she let it slip that Mr. Collins would attempt to 'persuade' you to accept him again. Fearing what tactics Collins might employ, I rode as fast as I could. And it appears my concern was warranted." He looked rather grimly at Collins.

"I compromised her! She must marry me." Despite cowering on the floor, Mr. Collins had a somewhat triumphant smile on his face. Had that been his aim all along?

Elizabeth placed her hand on William's arm in case he tried to strike the other man again, but her fiancé simply laughed. "I compromised her first, Collins! I have a prior claim." She glanced surreptitiously toward the hallway, fearful who might hear. Fortunately, the door was closed.

Mr. Collins stared, scandalized, at William. "You-you—"

William put his arm around Elizabeth's waist and pulled her close. "Yes, it is true. I kissed her on the terrace at Pemberley." He shrugged. "So I shall simply have to marry her." He shot a meaningful look at Collins. "And I suggest that *you* find the road to Kent as quickly as possible. There is nothing for you here."

Mr. Collins seemed somehow to grow smaller. "Y-yes, yes. I do think that is…well, that is to say…Lady Catherine will want me to…" He continued stammering out nonsense, but William turned away from him and guided Elizabeth toward the door with a hand on her back.

The hand fell away as Elizabeth opened the door and stepped into the hallway, but she could feel William hovering behind her protectively. Elizabeth's mother, Kitty, and Mary were huddled near the door. Clearly, they had been attempting to listen in to the conversation in the drawing room, although Elizabeth doubted they had heard much.

Mama's hands were all aflutter. "Lizzy, what has happened? Mr. Darcy arrived, Jane told him where you were, and then he rushed in. We heard the strangest sounds!" Kitty's and Mary's heads bobbed in agreement.

Elizabeth cleared her throat. "Mr. Darcy and Mr. Collins had a bit of a quarrel, Mama, but I think it has been resolved."

"A quarrel!" Her mother looked positively scandalized. "But I thought Mr. Collins would propose again!"

Behind Elizabeth, Mr. Darcy made a noise that was almost a growl. Surely Elizabeth's face was bright red by this point! How had her love life become such a public spectacle?

"Actually, Mama, that was the source of the quarrel. Mr. Collins did make me another offer." Her mother's face lit up at this news. "But I was forced to decline it."

"Elizabeth!" her mother exclaimed. "Why in heaven's name would you do such a thing? We shall be turned out into the hedgerows! And then we shall—" Her mother's tirade continued in this vein. Elizabeth simply waited until she ran out of energy. It took some time. Finally, she regarded Elizabeth challengingly, hands on hips. "And what do you have to say about that, Lizzy?"

"I only have one thing to say. And that is that I could not accept Mr. Collins because I am engaged to Mr. Darcy."

Mrs. Bennet was silent a full minute. Then her mother emitted an ear-splitting shriek. "Mr. Bennet! Mr. Bennet!"

Her father emerged from his study with admirable alacrity. "You shrieked, my dear?"

"Lizzy is engaged to Mr. Darcy!"

"Yes, I know. I gave my permission a fortnight ago." Mr. Bennet winked at Elizabeth.

"And you said nothing of it in your letters to me?"

He removed his glasses and cleaned them with his handkerchief. "No, my dear. I thought it best to deliver the news in person. Nor did I write to you about Jane's engagement to Mr. Bingley."

"Jane! Mr. Bingley!" Her mother was practically hyperventilating. "And you said nothing?"

Having heard her name, Jane emerged from the kitchen into the hallway. "Mama? Did you want me?"

Her mother stepped forward and enveloped Jane in a hug. "Mr. Bingley!" Then she turned back to Elizabeth, still a little dumbfounded. "Mr. Darcy!" She blinked rapidly. "Mr. Bingley, Mr. Darcy! I shall go distracted!" For a moment, she appeared in danger of swooning.

Jane took her arm. "Mama, perhaps we should discuss my trousseau?"

"Oh, yes! We must work on it at once! And Lizzy must have one as well…" Jane managed to steer her into the kitchen, and finally, silence reigned in the hallway.

Her father replaced his spectacles on his nose and then peered at Kitty and Mary. "When you two get engaged, I beg you to do so quietly. This has been very hard on my poor nerves." He smiled at them all and then retired once more to his study.

Elizabeth's sisters each gave her congratulatory hugs before running up the stairs giggling and chatting, leaving her alone in the hallway with Mr. Darcy.

"Oh!" Elizabeth's hand flew to her mouth. "I just now remembered Mr. Collins. We should get him out of Longbourn as quickly as possible."

William cleared his throat. "I actually took the liberty of looking in on the drawing room a moment ago. Collins is gone. My guess it that he took advantage of the…excitement with your mother to make good his escape."

"Thank goodness!"

"Hmm…indeed," he murmured, glancing around the empty hallway, "although I am sorry he will not witness this." He gave her a wicked smile.

"Witness what?"

He pulled her into his arms. "I am taking this opportunity to compromise you once again." His lips brushed lightly over hers.

"Well, you do have the prior claim…" she murmured.

And William compromised her once more in a most delightful way.

Epilogue

"Your cousin appears to be limping," William murmured in Elizabeth's ear. As sweet nothings went, it was not the most romantic thing he had ever whispered to her, but he had just spent a full minute nuzzling her neck, so she could not accuse him of lacking ardor. He had taken the opportunity of an unguarded moment following their wedding ceremony to draw her into a nook under the Longbourn stairs to steal a kiss and lavish attention on that and other sensitive parts of her body.

As much as Elizabeth enjoyed—nay, relished—the attention, she had reluctantly called a halt so they could venture into the drawing room and greet the guests to the wedding breakfast.

She now was pouring tea, an occupation that prevented William from indulging in any more nuzzling, but he did not seem capable of leaving her side. Even now, he stood so close, his breath tickled her neck. Fortunately, few guests seemed to notice his excessive proximity, and those who did smiled knowingly. Elizabeth supposed newlywed couples could be granted some leeway.

Elizabeth poured a cup for her sister, Mary, as she observed Mr. Collins slowly lurching across the drawing room. Neither she nor William had wished to invite her cousin to the wedding, but her mother had been insistent. "He does seem to be favoring one leg. I wonder what happened," Elizabeth agreed.

"Oh!" Mary's hand flew to her mouth, and she blushed red. "I stomped on his foot."

"Mary!"

Her sister's expression shifted rapidly from contrite to defiant. "He tried to kiss me!"

"He did what?" William growled.

"I do not believe he will try it again." Mary unsuccessfully stifled a giggle. "He asked me to marry him and then tried to kiss me before giving me an opportunity to respond. He would not release me, so I stomped on his foot as hard as I could."

"He asked you to marry him?" Elizabeth repeated, aghast.

Mary nodded. "I believe he feels he must choose someone from our family."

Elizabeth's eyes widened. "Perhaps we ought to warn Kitty."

"I did," Mary said, a touch smugly. "She arranged for some protection."

Protection? What on earth did Mary...? Elizabeth glanced over at Kitty and saw Colonel Fitzwilliam, quite dashing in his regimentals, hovering protectively next to her. As Mr. Collins limped past, the colonel watched him intently, but the parson continued walking.

William chuckled. "I hope Richard does not mind being pressed into service." As Elizabeth watched, Kitty and the colonel exchanged broad smiles.

"No, I do not believe he minds," Mary said, with a grin of her own.

"If Mr. Collins approaches you again, please tell me, Mary." William regarded her intently. "I will ensure he leaves you alone."

Mary smiled as she lowered her tea cup. "I do not believe he will approach me again. However, he is staying at Lucas Lodge. Perhaps he has some hopes of Charlotte."

"Charlotte?" Elizabeth exclaimed.

"She is not terribly romantic, you know Lizzy," Mary observed. "Mr. Collins could offer a comfortable home to someone who is in danger of becoming an old maid."

"Hmm...I do not know how much of a danger that is..." William tilted his head meaningfully toward a corner of the room where Charlotte Lucas was sharing a plate of biscuits and laughing with the Meryton curate, Mr. Browning, who had performed their wedding ceremony.

The man was new to Hertfordshire but seemed pleasant and thoughtful and would make an excellent husband for Charlotte.

"Good for her!" Elizabeth smiled. "She deserves better than Mr. Collins."

"Don't we all?" Mary asked, smiling.

"Indeed." Elizabeth shuddered at the thought of how close she had come to marrying the man.

"Oh, there is Maria! I must tell her my story." Mary hurried away.

Elizabeth looked up at her new husband. "If not for you, I might be Mrs. Collins."

He shook his head, looking miserable. "Do not say such things, my love. I still have nightmares in which I arrive at Longbourn and find you married to him."

She rested her hand on his forearm. "I am sorry, I did not mean to distress you."

He reached out a hand to delicately stroke her face. "I am certain such dreams will fade—now that it is quite impossible. Now that you are Mrs. *Darcy*."

She gave him a soft, grateful smile. "Yes, I am very fortunate you rescued me."

William cupped her face with his palm. "No, Elizabeth, you do not understand. You do not know what my life would be like without you. It is *you* who rescued *me*."

The End

About Victoria Kincaid

As a professional freelance writer, Victoria writes about IT, data storage, home improvement, green living, alternative energy, and healthcare. Some of her more…unusual writing subjects have included space toilets, taxi services, laser gynecology, bidets, orthopedic shoes, generating energy from onions, Ferrari rental car services, and vampire face lifts (she swears she is not making any of this up).

Victoria has a Ph.D. in English literature and has taught composition to unwilling college students. Today she teaches business writing to willing office professionals and tries to give voice to the demanding cast of characters in her head. She lives in Virginia with her husband, two children who love to read, and an overly affectionate cat. A lifelong Jane Austen fan, Victoria confesses to an extreme partiality for the Colin Firth miniseries version of *Pride and Prejudice.*

Thank you for purchasing this book.

Your support makes it possible for authors like me to continue writing.

Please consider leaving a review where you purchased the book

or at Goodreads.com.

Learn more about me and my upcoming releases:

Website: www.victoriakincaid.com

Twitter: VictoriaKincaid@kincaidvic

Blog: https://kincaidvictoria.wordpress.com/

Facebook: https://www.facebook.com/kincaidvictoria

The Secrets of Darcy and Elizabeth

Victoria Kincaid

In this *Pride and Prejudice* variation, a despondent Darcy travels to Paris in the hopes of forgetting the disastrous proposal at Hunsford. Paris is teeming with English visitors during a brief moment of peace in the Napoleonic Wars, but Darcy's spirits don't lift until he attends a ball and unexpectedly encounters…Elizabeth Bennet! Darcy seizes the opportunity to correct misunderstandings and initiate a courtship.

Their moment of peace is interrupted by the news that England has again declared war on France, and hundreds of English travelers must flee Paris immediately. Circumstances force Darcy and Elizabeth to escape on their own, despite the risk to her reputation. Even as they face dangers from street gangs and French soldiers, romantic feelings blossom during their flight to the coast. But then Elizabeth falls ill, and the French are arresting all the English men they can find….

When Elizabeth and Darcy finally return to England, their relationship has changed, and they face new crises. However, they have secrets they must conceal—even from their own families.

Amazon Top 10 Bestseller in Regency Romance

Amazon Top 10 Hot New Release in Regency Romance

Average of 4 stars on Amazon (more than 120 reviews)

Pride and Proposals

Victoria Kincaid

What if Mr. Darcy's proposal was too late?

Darcy has been bewitched by Elizabeth Bennet since he met her in Hertfordshire. He can no longer fight this overwhelming attraction and must admit he is hopelessly in love.

During Elizabeth's visit to Kent she has been forced to endure the company of the difficult and disapproving Mr. Darcy, but she has enjoyed making the acquaintance of his affable cousin, Colonel Fitzwilliam.

Finally resolved, Darcy arrives at Hunsford Parsonage prepared to propose—only to discover that Elizabeth has just accepted a proposal from the Colonel, Darcy's dearest friend in the world.

As he watches the couple prepare for a lifetime together, Darcy vows never to speak of what is in his heart. Elizabeth has reason to dislike Darcy, but finds that he haunts her thoughts and stirs her emotions in strange ways.

Can Darcy and Elizabeth find their happily ever after?

Please enjoy an excerpt on the following page....

Pride and Proposals

Chapter 1

Miss Bennet, I must tell you that almost since our first ...

No. Too formal.

You must be aware of my attentions ...

Would that assume too much?

You must allow me to tell you how much I admire you ...

This came closest to expressing his sentiments, but would she view it as excessive?

Darcy guided his stallion along the path to Hunsford Parsonage, anxiety increasing by the minute. Somehow the perfect words for a proposal must come to mind. He was close by the parsonage.

Almost out of time.

He took a deep breath. The master of Pemberley was unaccustomed to such agitation of the mind. But Elizabeth Bennet had a habit of unsettling his nerves as no one else could. Not for the first time, he wondered why that should indicate she would be the ideal companion of his future life. However, he had wrestled with his sentiments all day and finally concluded that it must be so, despite his objections to her family.

He had not slept the night previous and only fitfully the night before that. Practically his every thought was occupied by Elizabeth Bennet. Every minute of the day, he would recall a pert response she had made to his aunt or a piece of music she had played on the pianoforte. Or the sparkle of life in her fine eyes.

Yes, at first she had seemed an unlikely candidate for the mistress of Pemberley, but his passion could not be denied.

He no longer made the attempt.

Strange. He had been angered with himself for months that he could not rid himself of this ... obsession with Miss Bennet. But once he had determined to surrender to the sentiment and propose to her, he felt almost ... happy. Despite the fleeting sensations of guilt and doubt, he could not help but imagine how joyful it would be to have her as his wife.

He pictured the expression on Elizabeth's face when he declared himself. Undoubtedly, she was aware of his admiration, and she had returned his flirtatious banter on more than one occasion, but she could have no serious hopes for an alliance. Her delight would make any of his misgivings worth it.

The woods on either side of the path thinned, and Darcy slowed his horse to a walk as he reached the clearing surrounding the parsonage. Initially, he had been bitterly disappointed when Elizabeth's headache had prevented her from accompanying the Collinses to Rosings for tea, but then he recognized a perfect opportunity to speak with her alone.

Excusing himself from the gathering had not presented any difficulties. His cousin, Colonel Fitzwilliam, had received a letter that day with word of an unexpected inheritance of property following the death of his mother's sister. Darcy was well pleased for his cousin, who had chafed at the limitations of a second son's life. Richard had excused himself to plan for an immediate departure from Rosings the next day so he could soon visit his new estate. Darcy had seized on the excuse as well – since, naturally, he would be taking Richard in his coach and would necessarily need to prepare.

Darcy turned his thoughts to the task at hand.

You must allow me to tell you how violently I admire ...

No.

You must allow me to tell you how ardently I admire and love you ...

Perhaps …

Darcy swung his leg over the pommel and slid off his saddle, tying his horse up at a post outside the Collinses' front door. Pausing for a moment, he breathed deeply, willing his body to calmness. Then he seized the door knocker and rapped.

The maid who answered the door appeared unnecessarily flustered. As he followed her down the short hallway to the Collinses' modest drawing room, Darcy had a dawning sense of wrongness.

Voices already emanated from the drawing room. Darcy immediately recognized Elizabeth's lovely soprano. But the other voice was male, too muffled for him to hear. Had Collins returned home unexpectedly?

Darcy quickened his stride, almost crowding against the maid as she opened the drawing room door. "Mr. Darcy, ma'am," the maid announced before swiftly scurrying away.

Darcy blinked several times. His mind had difficulty understanding what his eyes saw. His cousin Fitzwilliam was in the drawing room. With Elizabeth. With *Darcy's* Elizabeth. In actuality, Richard sat beside her on the settee, almost indecently close.

Why is Richard here? Darcy wondered with some irritation. *Should he not be packing for his departure rather than preventing me from proposing?*

Richard and Elizabeth had been smiling at each other, but now both regarded Darcy in surprise.

For a moment, all was silence. Darcy could hear the crackling of logs in the fireplace. He had the nagging sensation of having missed something of importance but could not identify it.

"I … uh … came to inquire after your health, Miss Bennet." Given the circumstances, Darcy was proud that the words emerged at all coherently.

"I am feeling much recovered, thank you." Her voice was somewhat breathless.

A look passed between Richard and Elizabeth, and she gave a tiny nod. Darcy's sense of mystification increased. Finally, Richard sprang to his feet with a huge grin on his face. "Darcy, you arrived at just the right moment. You can be the first to congratulate me." At that moment, Darcy started to get a sinking, gnawing feeling in the pit of his stomach. "Elizabeth has consented to be my wife!"

Chapter 2

Elizabeth opened her eyes, staring at the canopy of her bed, unwilling to face the business of donning clothing and descending for breakfast just yet. She wished to review and savor her memories of the previous day's events before facing others' reactions.

A chance encounter with Colonel Fitzwilliam the previous day had revealed the distressing news that Mr. Darcy had conspired with Mr. Bingley's sisters to separate Jane from their brother. The anguish that followed had brought about a headache, preventing her attendance at Rosings for tea.

Elizabeth had been grateful for a reprieve from Mr. Darcy's company, being uncertain if she could treat him civilly. Instead, she had occupied her time reviewing Jane's recent letters, noting how out-of-spirits her sister's words sounded. Although Jane wrote nothing in particular to elicit concern, her entire manner lacked the enthusiasm her sister usually displayed. As Elizabeth peered out of the window, worrying that her sister might never recover her spirits, the maid had announced Colonel Fitzwilliam's arrival.

Initially, the colonel entered and settled on a chair near the fireplace, only to vacate it and wander about the room. They spoke of inconsequential matters: her health and that of her family. Elizabeth found herself concerned about the colonel's health. He displayed a kind of nervous energy that she had never before encountered in him.

Finally, he settled once more in a chair, leaning forward so that his eyes caught and held hers in an intense gaze. When Elizabeth had first met the colonel, she had thought him pleasant, but not handsome. Now she was forced to reevaluate this opinion. The energy that lit his face transformed it; she could not tear her gaze away.

"I received a letter today." He paused, and Elizabeth nodded. "My mother's sister, Rebecca Tilbury, died unexpectedly last week."

"I am sorry to hear it." Elizabeth was mystified about the import of this conversation; he did not appear to be mourning his aunt's passing.

The colonel waved away her concern. "I barely knew her. My family was not on good terms with her, and I had not seen her since my boyhood. The letter I received was from her solicitor. The terms of her will stipulate that I am to inherit her estate of Hargrave Manor. It is only an hour's ride from my parents' home in Matlock." His eyes were unfocused as he contemplated the vagaries of fate and capricious relations. "I did not expect it."

After a moment, the colonel returned his attention to Elizabeth. "The estate is quite good. Several hundred acres, producing a steady income of some four thousand a year." Elizabeth nodded and smiled. "And a house in Town as well. I will sell my commission immediately so that I may take possession and manage the estate."

"I am very happy for you. This is good fortune!" she said warmly. Now Elizabeth better understood why the colonel appeared so abstracted. He was coming to terms with his unexpected good fortune. However, why was he sharing the news with her now? Surely it could have waited until she visited Rosings on the morrow?

Colonel Fitzwilliam's eyes fixed on Elizabeth's face, provoking a blush from her. "Today, when we walked in the Park, I told you that younger sons did not have the luxury of marrying where they would like."

Elizabeth's breath caught.

"This thought has often tormented me this week. More than once I considered ignoring the needs of an income to follow the dictates of my heart. But today, I need not make such a choice. I can marry where I would. And I would marry you, Miss Bennet, if you would have me."

Elizabeth's whole body flushed. Thankfully, she was already seated, or she might have fallen. She opened her mouth, but no words emerged. This was the most unexpected event. Well, no, the *most* unexpected would be a proposal from Mr. Darcy. She almost laughed at the thought.

The colonel scrutinized her face anxiously, his hands absently kneading the gloves in his lap. "I can perceive that I have surprised you. Do not feel compelled to give me a response immediately."

Elizabeth swallowed and found her voice. "Yes. That is, yes, this is a surprise." Why was her throat suddenly so dry? Every word was hoarse to her ears. "Such an honor is quite unexpected." Her mind was in turmoil as she attempted to sort through her feelings about the man before her.

"Miss Bennet, let me assure you of my sincerest affection." He reached out across the space separating them and boldly took her hand in his. "Never have I encountered a woman who I felt would suit me so well. Your wit and vivacity—indeed, your spirit—are ..." He swallowed hard and glanced at the fireplace. "To be honest, words fail me. I am a soldier, not an orator. But should you honor me with your hand, I will do everything in my power to make you happy."

In truth, Elizabeth had not allowed herself to consider him as a potential husband. An earl's son, no matter how impoverished he believed himself, was considerably beyond her expectations. But now that she reflected on their, albeit brief, association she recognized he was one of the most amiable men of her acquaintance. He was unfailingly charming and affable, polite to his aunt and cousins, even when they were at their most vexing.

When all Mr. Darcy would do was stare at Elizabeth in disapproval, Colonel Fitzwilliam would talk to her with great animation, eager to learn about her family and the country around Longbourn. Despite their short acquaintance, she was aware they shared remarkably similar tastes in books and music—and always anticipated their conversations with great pleasure.

Elizabeth had always expected to marry for love, but she fully recognized the precariousness of her family's situation. Someone in her family must marry well, or their circumstances would be dire indeed when Mr. Collins inherited Longbourn. Jane seemed so out of spirits over Mr. Bingley's rejection that Elizabeth wondered if she would ever wish to attract another man's attention. And Elizabeth was loathe to trust her family's future to the whims of her younger sisters. Goodness knows what type of husband Kitty or Lydia would bring home!

She did not love Colonel Fitzwilliam, but she believed she *could* love him upon greater acquaintance. No other man had so provoked her interest since the early days of her acquaintance with Mr. Wickham. And, she realized with no little surprise, she was rather more disposed to the colonel than she had ever been to Wickham. There was a certain openness in the colonel's character, a selflessness, which she very much admired.

He provoked laughter from her far more than any other man she had ever encountered, which she considered quite a recommendation. Surely laughter was an excellent basis for friendship, and friendship a good start for a marriage, she reasoned. She could live a long time and never meet a man who suited her as well as the colonel.

"Miss Bennet?" Colonel Fitzwilliam's eyebrows had drawn together, creating a crease in the middle of his forehead. He must have been awaiting her response for some time.

"Forgive me, Colonel, you have given me much to think about."

He stood. "I should leave you to your thoughts. I have no desire to rush your decision."

At the sight of the colonel moving toward the door, Elizabeth realized what her decision would be. In fact, the decision had already been made.

She rushed across the room, wishing to intercept the colonel before he reached the door. "No, please do not leave. Richard, stay."

At the sound of his Christian name on her lips, the colonel turned to face her. His eyes sought hers, alight with hope.

"Yes." She smiled gently at him. "My answer is yes."

Richard's face broke into a wide smile. "Ah, Elizabeth, you have made me the happiest man in England! Nay, the whole world!"

She laughed softly. He caught her hand in his, and she realized with a shock that neither of them was wearing gloves. The feeling of his warm flesh against the sensitive skin of her hand felt deliciously forbidden, almost as if they had been caught kissing.

"Darling," he murmured and pulled her gently against his chest. Her head nestled just under his chin, a perfect fit. Yes, she could be quite happy with the Col— Richard. Perhaps she was a fair way to being in love with him already.

After a moment, Richard broke off the embrace, regarding her seriously. "Tomorrow, I must ride to Longbourn and call on your father. When would you like the wedding to take place?" He took her hand and led her over to the settee, sitting daringly close to her.

And so Mr. Darcy discovered them a quarter of an hour later.

Chapter 3

If someone wished to devise a personal hell specifically for him, Darcy mused, they could not possibly create a better one. He stood at the foot of the stairs to Colonel Fitzwilliam's new London townhouse. It was not as grand as Darcy House and the neighborhood was not quite as fashionable, but it was certainly elegant and spacious enough for a second son who, until three weeks ago, had no expectations of aspiring to any accommodations beyond a set of rooms to let.

Darcy regarded the house's impressive neo-Classical façade. He had been anticipating this day with all the joy most people might give a raging fever. Now that he had arrived, somehow his legs had turned to lead and would not obey his instructions to climb the stairs.

Even a simple glance at the townhouse caused dread to curl into a tight knot in his stomach. How would he survive the evening with his dignity intact? No, that was beyond hope. How would he survive the evening at all?

His eyes closed briefly, blocking the view of the offending structure. Darcy had quit Rosings the morning after Fitzwilliam's awful announcement. Fortunately, Darcy's plans had already been fixed, so no one thought his swift departure odd, and Richard apparently perceived no strangeness in Darcy's manner. *Perhaps he should consider a career on the stage.*

Richard's letters had described how he had traveled to Hertfordshire, easily securing Mr. Bennet's consent to the marriage, and then returned to Hunsford where he escorted Elizabeth to her uncle's house in London. In the intervening weeks, Richard had sold his commission and visited his estate, attending to all the urgent matters involved in taking immediate possession. Meanwhile, Elizabeth and her aunt made preparations for a wedding scheduled for some three months hence.

Darcy had tortured himself by quite thoroughly perusing each of Richard's letters, absorbing every detail of his cousin's felicity with Elizabeth. Bizarrely, he almost preferred to hear news of her—even when it concerned her betrothal to another man—than to know nothing of her life, a true sign of how pathetic his obsession had become.

He had tried—oh, how he had tried!—to resume his former indifference toward Elizabeth. However, now he had confessed his feelings to himself, the genie refused to return into the lamp. In a moment of honesty, during one of many nights spent staring at his ceiling, Darcy admitted to himself that he had never been truly indifferent to Elizabeth. When he had thought himself indifferent, he had only been fooling himself.

Darcy could only count one slim success in his favor over the past weeks. Since returning from Hunsford, he had adroitly avoided both Richard and Elizabeth.

Until today.

Richard was hosting a dinner so his family could be better acquainted with Elizabeth's. Darcy could not escape the invitation.

He had considered inventing urgent business at Pemberley. Or a sudden illness. Despite Darcy's abhorrence of disguise, these thoughts held alarming appeal, but finally, he had conceded the necessity of facing the happy couple eventually. Prolonging the inevitable smacked of cowardice—and he had faults enough without adding to them.

Darcy opened his eyes. He might as well be a French nobleman facing the guillotine. Perhaps cowardice had something to recommend it.

His stomach churned sickeningly, and his hands were wet with perspiration inside his gloves. But there was nothing for it. He must go. He willed his feet to climb the steps, one at a time, until he reached the porch, having failed to be struck down by a conveniently timed meteor.

His knock was answered almost immediately by a smartly dressed footman who took Darcy's coat and ushered him into Richard's study. Darcy saw no sign of other guests.

Richard glanced up with a smile when Darcy entered. He was seated behind a massive oaken desk, every inch the industrious landowner. "Darcy, good to see you!" He maneuvered around the desk to shake Darcy's hand and gestured toward to a couple of elegant chairs near the fireplace. "Brandy?" Richard asked. Darcy nodded; spirits could only help him survive the night.

Richard poured two glasses from a crystal decanter and handed one to Darcy before taking his seat. "I am pleased you have the opportunity to see the house," Richard remarked.

Was that a subtle suggestion that Darcy might have visited sooner? Well, Darcy supposed he would have visited more than once by now were it not for his cousin's engagement. "It is an elegant residence," Darcy said. "I hope you are pleased with it."

"Oh, quite," Fitzwilliam said. "It is nothing to Darcy House, of course, but far superior to my set of apartments."

"Indeed." Darcy admired the room's large marble fireplace, happy to have a neutral topic of conversation.

"The furnishings are a bit out of fashion, but Elizabeth will have the opportunity to redecorate as she wishes." *Ah, so much for neutrality.* Darcy suppressed his flinch at the mention of her name but finished his brandy in one gulp. "Where are the other guests?"

"I invited you here early. I wished to speak with you privately."

"Oh?" Without waiting for Richard's assistance, Darcy rose and visited the sideboard to refill his brandy glass.

"About Elizabeth."

Darcy froze in place. *Could his cousin suspect something?* He willed himself to act normally, but his hand shook, and he spilled a small puddle of brandy, cursing under his breath.

Richard peered over. "Never mind. The servants will clean."

Having poured a generous amount of brandy on his second attempt, Darcy gulped, hoping to calm the coil of anxiety in his stomach. He sank back into his seat, regarding his cousin warily.

Richard was rubbing his hands together, gazing absentmindedly at the window. Darcy believed he had been successful in concealing his feelings for Elizabeth, but Richard knew him better than anyone. Perhaps he had guessed.

Darcy stared into the fire. He could do nothing but admit the truth. There was nothing he could say in his own defense, even though such an admission might irreparably damage his friendship with Richard irreparably. Damn!

How had they come to this pass? He valued Richard's friendship above all others.

Finally, Richard sighed heavily. "Elizabeth believes you do not like her."

"Pardon?" Darcy's hand jerked, and he almost spilled more brandy. Surely he had not heard aright.

Richard's expression was somewhat apologetic. "She … believes you do not approve of her family and find fault with her behavior."

Darcy pulled his gaze from his cousin's face and stared at the window next to the fireplace, suppressing the temptation to laugh. Only he was in a position to appreciate the irony. "No… I …." Darcy's voice was choked. "That is not the case at all."

"So I told her. I said you disapprove of most people, and even those who meet your approval often see you as proud and distant."

Darcy grimaced. "I thank you kindly for that endorsement of my character."

Richard shrugged unapologetically. Darcy rapidly reviewed his carefully stored memories of his conversations with Elizabeth. How had he created such a misimpression?

Unable to look at his cousin, he fixed his eyes on the inch of brandy in his glass. "I do not disapprove of Miss Bennet at all. I believe you have made an excellent choice." God willing, Richard would never know *how* excellent. "Her family's situation is unfortunate and some of her relatives can be … difficult …"

Richard chuckled. "I *have* been to Longbourn," he said drily.

Darcy chose each word carefully. "But I believe Miss Bennet to be of superior understanding and excellent conversation. I am often of a taciturn disposition in company, you know this."

His cousin grinned. "Yes. But I have known you my whole life. Elizabeth believes you spent the greater part of your visit at Rosings staring at her disapprovingly."

Thank God Richard remained ignorant of the true reason for those stares. That would make the situation intolerable. Well, more intolerable.

Richard stood and used the poker to idly rearrange the logs in the fireplace. It had been unseasonably cold for April, and the room was cooling rapidly as the fire died. "There is more." Darcy's gut clenched in apprehension. "Elizabeth's opinion of you was influenced by lies provided by Wickham during his time in Meryton."

Darcy let loose an oath, startling his cousin.

He had believed nothing would be worse than the revelation that she thought he disliked her. But now he found that when he thought she flirted and teased him at Rosings, she thought him a blackguard and could not wait to escape his company.

Darcy rubbed his face with one hand. He hated that Elizabeth would give credence to Wickham's opinion on *any* topic, particularly himself. Truth be told, Darcy did not like the idea of Wickham breathing the same air as Elizabeth.

Despite being consumed with jealousy, Darcy reflected that he should be grateful she had chosen Richard, who would treat her honorably. At the Netherfield ball, she had appeared to be partial to Wickham; the thought of that alliance could not be borne.

Perhaps he should be grateful that Richard had proposed before Darcy had the opportunity. Apparently, he had saved Darcy from a very embarrassing situation. Somehow the thought was not comforting.

Richard leaned against the mantel, watching the flames dance in the hearth. "I corrected her misapprehension regarding your father's bequest and

Wickham's dissolute ways, but I said nothing about his imposition on Georgiana. I wanted your permission."

"Tell her." Darcy's voice was a growl. "She should know." Richard reacted to his vehemence with raised eyebrows. "I do not wish her to harbor any doubts about my character—or Wickham's perfidy." Although it hardly signified now, Darcy loathed the idea of Elizabeth thinking ill of him.

"Very well. I shall tell her."

Darcy seized the opportunity to voice another thought. "I hope Eliz—Miss Bennet will be a friend to Georgiana. She had been so withdrawn. Miss Bennet may be helpful in encouraging Georgiana to socialize in company. She should fully understand Georgiana's history." Of course, when Darcy had pictured Elizabeth helping Georgiana, he had imagined them as sisters, but cousins must suffice.

A broad smile spread over Richard's face. "An excellent suggestion, William! Georgiana only recently arrived from Pemberley, so they have not met. But I believe the acquaintance would be very beneficial to Georgiana. And to Elizabeth as well. Georgiana is one member of our family who might welcome her."

Darcy nodded his understanding. Fitzwilliam's letters had indicated how his parents had been unhappy at his rather precipitous choice of a "country miss" with no fortune. When Richard had refused their request to end the engagement, they had treated Elizabeth with little welcome.

"I hope you can demonstrate to Elizabeth that some of my family does not disapprove of our match." Richard watched Darcy carefully as he voiced the request.

Darcy suppressed inappropriate laughter; after all, he did disapprove—most strenuously. The irony was so thick it threatened to choke him.

His face must have betrayed this bewildering array of emotions. Richard was regarding him with consternation. "You are my oldest and dearest friend. I hope you can be a friend to my future wife."

Darcy closed his eyes briefly. If only Richard knew how friendly Darcy could be with Elizabeth! But apparently, he had given a performance worthy of a master thespian.

"I will do everything in my power to support this marriage." Darcy's vow was rewarded with a smile that almost made all the pain worthwhile. "I never intended to cause Miss Bennet discomfort and will endeavor to amend my behavior." The words sounded stiff and formal in Darcy's ears, but more emotion-laden language might betray too many of his secrets.

Darcy stared at his now-empty glass, wishing he could dare refill it. But there would be wine with dinner and then port after. Getting foxed held some appeal, but he might reveal too much to Richard—or, God forbid, Elizabeth—in an unguarded moment. Instead, he promised himself an evening of dissipation when he was safely home.

"Thank you." Richard's tone was warm as he strode over to his cousin and clapped him on the shoulder. He glanced at the clock on the mantel. "The other guests will arrive soon."

Darcy stood, straightening out his waistcoat and cravat. Despite recent events, he could not break the habit of looking his best for Elizabeth.

He followed his cousin to the door, but Richard turned before opening it. "Oh, I seated Elizabeth beside you at dinner, so you will have an opportunity to correct her misimpressions."

Darcy suppressed a groan. His cousin would have made an excellent medieval torturer. Darcy had anticipated that Elizabeth would sit adjacent to Richard and half a table away from himself. Then Darcy could gaze silently upon his beloved and pretend the smiles she bestowed on his cousin were actually for him.

Richard glanced over his shoulder as they exited the study, expecting a response. Darcy attempted to infuse his tone with enthusiasm. "Excellent."

Made in the USA
San Bernardino, CA
28 December 2015